The Temptation Project

Liminal Books

Liminal Books is an imprint of Between the Lines Publishing. The Liminal Books name and logo are trademarks of Between the Lines Publishing.

Cover design by Suzanne Johnson

Between the Lines Publishing
1769 Lexington Ave N., Ste 286
Roseville, MN 55113
btwnthelines.com

Published: April 2023

Original ISBN (Paperback) 978-1-958901-35-9

Original ISBN (eBook) 978-1-958901-36-6

The Temptation Project

By L.K. White

For my family, always my safe harbor

A Dangerous Flaw

She knew she wasn't going to be able to keep her problem hidden for much longer. The slightest misstep and it would be over. They'd turn her into a pile of ash. Pieces of her would drift around Hell forever.

Dragging herself into the conveyor and pushing the indicator button for Mantle II, Tarantula considered for the hundredth time how she might rid herself of the corruption growing within her. But she couldn't think of anywhere to turn. No one would take the time to fix a defective demon; it was easier to just make a new one.

The conveyor descended rapidly, then slowed to a stop. The door slid open with a soft whoosh. Tarantula reluctantly stepped out onto a platform that jutted into the broad cavern housing the Department of Torture. Smoke swirled up from below and curled into her nasal slits. Although the smell of fear and suffering had always been comforting to her in the past, now it filled her with foreboding. She turned to the left and trudged down the winding path leading to the lava pools that glowed an orange-red in the distance.

Skulking along the obsidian walkway, she barely noticed the shrieks and howls that used to give her such pleasure. She had come so far so fast, how could this be happening to her now? It wasn't so long ago that she had been created by the Department of Labor to serve as a lowly worker in the Department of Torture. Now she was the director of her own lava pit and winner of the prestigious Most Creative Torturer Award. Demons all over the Department of Torture envied her. Now her existence was in jeopardy.

As she passed under the broad stone archway of Lava Pit 103, the lagoons of bubbling magma that comprised her domain spread out before her, their connecting walkways like the links in a vast jeweled necklace. Surveying this always gave her a rush of pride. The Adolescent Torture Area was hers, she had created it, and no one would take it from her. She would cut out this poison before anyone was the wiser.

Glancing around, she saw none of her co-workers. Apparently, she had arrived so late that everyone had already entered their assigned soul containers. The green glow emanating from the cylindrical objects floating on multiple pools' surfaces confirmed that her demons were hard at work inside. Good. She didn't feel like talking to anyone anyway.

She climbed the steps of the stone crypt nearby that housed the daily Torture Assignment List. Once inside, she ran a claw listlessly down the names of the dead who would be attended to this session. There was a soul awaiting her in Lava Pool 39. Hmm, only one. The wiry hairs on the back of her neck bristled as she considered the list again. Had the Assignment Clerk noticed the change in quality of her torture narratives? Devil's damnation, her work had become shoddy. With a worried shake of the head, she grabbed a fresh torture module, exited the crypt, and began weaving her way between the steaming pools.

The small metal box felt light and smooth in her palm. Its design had been the basis for all of her success. Early on, she had been placed with a team of demons tasked with developing a method for tormenting souls directly within their storage containers. The Department of Torture was eager to accomplish this because it would save time (no more moving souls in and out each session), space (torture devices could be unwieldy), and cut down on the mess. When the breakthrough came and the prototype was tested and proven effective, Tarantula began a campaign to stealthily rob the credit from her teammates. Once she convinced the administration that she was the leader behind such a brilliant discovery, it took only moderate string-pulling to get herself selected to receive the Most Creative Torturer Award that year. She had been nursing the ambition to direct a torture area of her own, so the obvious next step while her fame lasted was to pester the High Council to allow her to create a specialized adolescent unit. She targeted that age group specifically because they had so many weaknesses and insecurities that thinking up ways to persecute them was both shockingly easy and infinitely entertaining. And, to be honest, the pediatric torture experts wanted nothing to do with teenage souls; they had a reputation for being quirky and irritating. And so the High Council eventually caved and Lava Pit 103 became hers.

A single dark container drifted aimlessly on the surface of Lava Pool 39. Tarantula squatted at the lagoon's edge and considered her grave situation. She had to face the fact that she hadn't created a decent torture narrative in months. After rocketing to fame, she had solidified her status by developing new intracontainer torture techniques. Simply put, Tarantula used information from souls' pasts to create stories that would force them to repeatedly experience their greatest fears played out in excruciating detail. Her technique was so popular that the wait list to work in the Adolescent Torture Area was remarkably long.

Now, for some unknown reason, she couldn't drum up torture scenarios that showcased her renowned malice. Actually, if any of her recent narratives came under departmental review, there would be no question that her reputation would collapse. And if they were to realize …. Her claws tightened around the lip of the pool. That could never happen. Today had to be the day. Right here, right now, she had to turn this thing around. Crossing her arms over her chest, lowering her chin, and winding her tail about her head, she shut her eye slits tightly. Concentrate, Tarantula. Make this soul truly suffer. After a moment she rose, cracked her neck, shook out her arms, and reached for the container. There was a satisfying snap when she fitted the module into place.

As she whirled through the interface and clicked on the green indicator light, she did a quick scan of the soul's Surface History imprinted on the container's inside wall (another of her excellent innovations). Ah, it appeared this soul enjoyed bullying others. Not one to waste his time studying, the soul had forced peers to do his homework and let him copy their answers during tests. Tarantula skipped down to the Demise section. One night, bored and restless, he had pressured two boys to come to his house while their parents were at a PTA meeting. Lucky for him, his father was too lazy to bother locking his gun cabinet. Earlier that day, the soul had selected a revolver and filled all six chambers with blanks. When the nervous boys showed up, he led them down to the basement, locked the door, and announced they were going to enjoy a game of Russian roulette together. As the boys sat frozen and terrified on the worn plaid sofa, he casually spun the revolver's cylinder and explained the rules. Then he handed the gun to the smaller of the two and ordered him to play. Pleading, crying, the boy slowly put the gun to his head and pulled the trigger.

Needless to say, the soul had not expected to see the kid crumple to the floor as a thin line of blood inched its way from his temple to his nostril. Who knew that shooting a blank at such close range could send the wadding from the cartridge into the idiot's head? Dumbfounded, the soul picked up the gun, brought it close to his face to examine it, and mistakenly fired the next blank through his eye and into his brain. The young boy survived; the bully did not.

Tarantula burst out laughing. Teenagers were so reliably stupid. She rubbed her hands together in eager anticipation of spinning this torture narrative. After probing the soul's memories, she easily recreated one of his prior classrooms and seated him between the same two boys he had lured to his basement. Then she assumed the form of his teacher, entered the narrative, and initiated the scenario with an announcement of a pop quiz. There was a flurry of paper and pencils as the students began answering the questions she had written on the blackboard. Just as the soul began craning his neck to look at his neighbor's work, her shadow crossed his desk.

"What exactly do you think you're doing?" she sneered, leaning in extra close to ensure that a reasonable quantity of spittle landed on his face. Without allowing him time to make an excuse, she lashed him with, "Do you know what we do to people who cheat at this school?"

She enjoyed his predictable response: the outbreak of sweat on the brow, a quickening of the breath and heartbeat, the satisfying dilation of his pupils. "You have no idea how much trouble you are in," she hissed in his ear.

While dragging him by the collar down the hall to the Principal's Office, the soul pleaded and groveled to a gratifying degree. She threw him in a chair in the outer office, warned him not to move, and stomped out of the door. Rematerializing in the inner office, she now took the form of the Principal. As she allowed a few additional moments for the soul's panic to fester, her mind drifted to imagining what it might be like to be an actual principal on The Surface. Why, someone in that position would have the delicious ability to truly torment teenagers. What damage could be incurred by administering just the right shame at the just the right moment. As she savored this, a small voice broke into her reverie. *What if,* it murmured, *this principal used her power to help this young man to see his own potential? To pursue a different path? Why, with a strong advocate ….*

Deafening sirens blasted into Tarantula's thoughts. She found herself sailing through air, then hitting the ground hard. Flashing red strobe lights blinded her. Slowly drawing herself up on her knees, she realized she must have somehow been ejected from the soul's container and thrown onto the pathway next to Lava Pool 39. In the pulsing light she could vaguely make out the charred cylinder floating at an odd angle on the pool's surface. Her right arm burned; focusing more closely, she saw that a chunk of melted module was stuck to her scales. After prying it off, she glanced around and noted more pieces of module scattered about. What had happened? She felt a sting in her left wing and winced while removing a shard of metal embedded in the delicate membrane. Just then, glaring white searchlights began crisscrossing the Adolescent Torture Area. The noise of the blaring sirens was unnerving. Great goblins, what was going on? As she tried to stand in the smoke and confusion, she felt strong talons grasp her upper arms and lift her into the air. Something huge and hairy was flying her somewhere fast. This was all very, very wrong.

A Meeting with The Maker

Down she was plunged in the heat and smoke, through caverns and passageways she had not known existed. The strong claws encircling Tarantula's arms bit painfully into her scales. She couldn't see much in the dim light as rock walls whirled past. The thunderous flapping of powerful wings above her drowned out all other sounds. Why had those sirens gone off and where was this thing carrying her? A hot wire of fear twisted inside of her.

She was flown through dark ravines and narrow tunnels, past stone valleys and lava rivers, far deeper into the earth than she had ever traveled. Her head ached and her arms were completely numb by the time her abductor landed with a thud on two huge feet and dropped her roughly on the ground. Before she could raise her head, the air whooshed around her and the unknown presence above lifted and vanished.

As the cloud of swirling ash around her slowly dissipated, she shakily stood. In front of her was a soaring wall of craggy gray rock that reached up and out of sight. A few yards away loomed a giant iron door set into the rock face. It was covered with some sort of sinuous design. Approaching it, she saw that the door was decorated with two serpents crafted out of metal that were entwined to form an enormous letter "L."

There was only one thing that letter could stand for. Her legs began to shake uncontrollably.

She turned to look for an escape, any route away from this terrifying entryway, when a hard poke at her back forced her forward. In the same moment, the door shuddered, and an opening appeared. A blast of sulfurous gas from within hit her in the face and burned the edges of her nasal slits. With no choice but to move ahead, she stepped across the threshold.

A few paces in placed her at the edge of a vast canyon surrounded by jagged walls that swept sharply downward. Peering over the ledge, she saw an orange-yellow glow that pulsated far below. Faint voices drifted up on the smoky air. She felt a second painful jab at her back and turned to find a small blue demon with red eyes silently gesturing with a pitchfork for her to proceed.

Where to go? She was too afraid to fly, too shaky to trust her wings. To her right she spied a stone pathway that appeared to lead downward. After another insistent nudge she began to make her way along the steep trail.

Steadying herself against boulders and stalagmites, she descended deeper into the cavern. Plumes of smoke rose out of cracks in the walls. The atmosphere was thick; everything was shrouded in a pungent yellow mist. She moved cautiously as she crossed bridges over boiling lava rivers and wound her way around geysers spewing scalding steam. Occasionally she stumbled and fell, only to feel the impatient pitchfork at her back prodding her to get up and move on. As she neared the canyon floor, the murmuring of voices grew louder and more distinct. She tried to focus her attention on taking the next step and not on what awaited her below.

As the path leveled and walking grew easier, she allowed herself a glimpse at her surroundings. The gray stone walls rising from the base of the canyon were no longer jagged, but polished to a glassy finish. Thick veins of gold cut across their smooth surfaces. Torches set high on the walls were supported by sconces decorated with shimmering gemstones. The path under her feet was widening and the rough stone gave way to lustrous red granite. Tarantula sensed that she must be nearing her destination.

The air was smokier in the lower canyon. Squinting up ahead, she could see why. Not far off was a huge wall of flame. Drawing closer, she realized in the hazy light that the blazing barrier was actually a line of hulking guards made entirely of fire. She had never heard of beings like this in Hell. She froze in place, not daring to move closer, but then was shoved so forcefully from behind that she fell forward on her hands and knees. As she lifted her head, she saw that the fire guards had created an opening for her to pass. Shivering, cowering, she crawled between the blazing bodies, narrowing her eye slits against their glare.

On the other side of the fiery flank the smoke thinned somewhat and she could begin to make out her surroundings. As she slowly got to her feet she found herself in a vast hall of polished marble. A few yards away was the base of some sort of tall platform. Her eyes tracked its edges upward. High above the dais, seated on a towering throne carved out of luminous green crystal, was a massive demon glaring down at her.

Huge and magnificent, Lucifer surpassed any stories she had heard of his beauty and ferocity. She saw that she herself had been crafted in his image, yet the details of his form were beyond exquisite. His body was powerfully built, with bulging muscles covered by deep red scales that glinted like cut rubies in the firelight. His elegant hands were tipped with curved, glistening black talons. Wrapped around the base of the throne was a long, tapering tail that ended in a precise barb. Although his wings were folded against his sides, given their immense height and large veining she could envision their majesty and strength once unfurled. Atop his head were two gleaming, ivory-colored horns. But by far his most arresting feature was his face; sharply sculpted and perfectly malevolent.

"Tarantula," he growled in a deep, resonant voice that reverberated against the surrounding walls, "what have you done?"

A violent quaking took over her body and she threw herself on the ground before him.

"How could you have allowed this to occur in Hell? In my Hell?"

She tried to bury her face in the ash.

"Stand up and face me!"

The pitchfork again, prodding as she forced herself upright.

"Answer me!"

Tarantula tried to speak but was only successful in generating a small puff of smoke.

"I'll tell you what happened. You, of all demons, created a torture narrative that suggested your soul receive ... oh, for Hell's sake, I can't say the word aloud, it's too disgusting. Your narrative, in the pit you direct, was creating an atmosphere of … ah, another H word that must never be uttered in my domain! What excuse could you possibly give to justify such outrageous and intolerable behavior? You, a decorated torturer!"

She struggled to think back to the moments right before the sirens and searchlights went off. What had she been doing? Let's see, she was creating the new narrative for the soul with the ridiculous Russian roulette story. She had dumped him in the outer office while she prepared for her role as his principal, and then she …. No, no, no, not that, please not that.

Tarantula realized, in that one quiet, vulnerable moment in the principal's office, that she had allowed her dangerous flaw, the insufferable tinge of sympathy that had begun to infiltrate her thoughts, to contaminate her torture narrative. She had infected it with hope.

"My liege," she begged, her hands extended upward in a gesture of supplication as she scrambled to come up with something, anything to say that might delay the inevitable.

"Don't you 'my liege' me," Lucifer snapped." How could you allow this? You, a winner of the Most Creative Torturer Award! You, who wanted to be our 'adolescent torture specialist.' Didn't I reward your work by authorizing the High Council to grant you your own lava pit? And this is how you repay me? By having a soul enjoy himself in Hell?"

"But...," she started again.

"There are no buts! This is Hell! What could you possibly have been thinking?"

Tarantula's head had cleared sufficiently for her to appreciate that if she didn't use her wits now there would be no second chance.

"Your Diabolicalness, please allow this most humble servant a word," she pleaded.

Lucifer sat back on his throne. His outburst had tired him. "Go ahead," he muttered.

Think fast, think fast, Tarantula.

"Oh, Great One, the only reason I was created was to serve you. I have faithfully worked as a torturer to make you proud."

Where was this going? How could she distract him from the truth?

"You have given me many rewards," she stalled, "and have honored me by instructing the High Council to not only consider my ideas but to implement them. I have pleased you with the success of the Adolescent Torture Area?"

"Yes, confound it," Lucifer retorted. "That is why I am so frustrated with you! Any other demon would have been thrown into the Abyss by now."

Tarantula took a deep breath to steady herself and continued. "Today's mishap was egregious, Evil One, and it will never happen again. But the reason it occurred is that I was deeply distracted by a new concept I am developing that far outshines any inventions I have created to date."

Steady now, Tarantula, sound like you know what you're talking about.

"And that concept is?"

"I have recently noticed a serious decline in the number of souls condemned to the Adolescent Torture Area. This is a concerning problem, but one that I believe can be remedied. With more focused temptation up on The Surface, we will be able to bring many more teenage souls to Hell."

Lucifer uncrossed and then recrossed his finely chiseled legs. Thin wisps of smoke escaped from his nostrils.

"More teenagers in Hell? Continue."

This could be her means of escape. She had long been curious about The Surface, and a trip up there would give her time to evade prying eyes in Hell while she worked through this wretched problem of hers. She glanced up. Lucifer was still glaring at her. Make this good, Tarantula, your existence depends on it.

"Although there is temptation on The Surface for teenagers, there could be more. Much more. If we were to train demons to exploit the tasks of adolescence which include the development of independence, identity ...."

"Don't dish out your adolescent claptrap to me, Tarantula," Lucifer said in an exasperated tone while flicking a hand dismissively in her direction. "The High Council had to endure it when you pitched your specialty torture pit idea, and I heard endless grumbling from them about you as a result. Exactly what are you suggesting?"

"Send me to The Surface," she said with conviction. "Let me mingle with the adolescents there. I have a deep knowledge of their weaknesses and understand their motivations. I can tempt them to sin and will provide you with more teenage souls than ever before. Consider this an experiment. If it works, we can train other demons to follow in my footsteps."

Lucifer heaved an exaggerated sigh. "We already have a Department of Temptation, as you well know. It has been extremely effective to date." He began examining the polished claws of his right hand.

She was losing his attention. If she didn't sell this to him now, she could kiss everything good-bye.

"Yes, Sire, I am aware, but adolescents are at a formative time in their lives and with the correct management …."

Lucifer irritably cut her off. "And how would you pull off this 'mingling?' You don't even look human."

Tarantula desperately groped for a response, but she had nothing. In another second Lucifer would condemn her to the Abyss. It was hopeless.

"I will assist her, Your Evilness, if you will permit me," a strong voice called from out of the shadows.

A tall, dignified demon with a commanding presence boldly stepped into the open space before the dais.

"Beelzebub, Prince of Demons and faithful advisor, how does this business interest you?"

"My king," the demon bowed deeply. "As you know, I have spent a great deal of time on The Surface, and have intimate knowledge of the fallibility of humans. It is true that teenagers are a population we have not fully capitalized on. They are a weak-willed, vulnerable group that could be turned to the dark side with minimal intervention. I have followed Tarantula's work and I believe her idea has merit. Allow me to serve as her supervisor and mentor. It may bring you more souls, and will provide me with a welcomed diversion from my usual responsibilities on The Surface. Call this the 'Temptation Project' if you will. Should she fail, you can demote her to the Department of Lava Maintenance. That should quell any future trouble from her."

A quiet laugh rumbled in Lucifer's chest. After a pause, he shrugged.

"She is under your direction, then. I grant you six months to prove to me that this 'Temptation Project' of yours is of any worth. But on no account may her identity as a demon ever be disclosed to any being on The Surface. Beelzebub, I am entrusting you to ensure this is so. The consequences will be severe should this mandate be compromised."

"Yes, my lord," Beelzebub intoned, with another sweeping bow.

In a few graceful strides, Beelzebub crossed the marble expanse and came to a stop in front of Tarantula. Looking down at her with piercing yellow eyes he murmured, "Come, Tarantula, we have much work to do."

Tarantula's mind was racing. She was unbelievably fortunate that Lucifer had been distracted from the cause of the explosion in Lava Pool 39. Miraculously, this high demon had stepped in and vouched for her plan. She was to go to The Surface and procure teenage souls for Lucifer, but how? Bloody boogers, she thought as she lifted off from the ground and flew after Beelzebub, what had she gotten herself into?

The Transformation

A great many things happened all at once. Upon her return to Lava Pit 103, Tarantula saw that someone had already cleaned up the mess from the exploded module and assigned the soul's container to another torturer. A representative from the High Council turned up almost immediately and informed her that she was being transferred to the Department of Temptation.

"What a stir you have caused, and in your own unit," she remarked in a snippy tone. "We've had to schedule support sessions for all Adolescent Torture Area workers as everyone is so shaken by what took place. Nightshade will replace you as director. Never before have we had to deal with such an unseemly situation."

Co-workers were shocked to see Tarantula return. Rumors were rampant.

"We heard you were vaporized," one of her assistants said.

"Someone told me you were thrown into the Abyss," another commented.

"Should have been," a particularly prickly demon muttered under her breath.

She was asked what happened, where she was taken, and what punishment she received. But Beelzebub had coached her to be vague in her responses and to mention absolutely nothing about her meeting with Lucifer and the project she was about to undertake. He relocated her to a comfortable crevice within the Department of Temptation. "Out of sight, out of mind," he observed.

It took very little time for Tarantula to realize how fortunate she was to have Beelzebub as an ally. She doubted she would have survived her meeting with Lucifer without his intervention, and now she couldn't imagine how she would have carried out planning for the Temptation Project without his assistance. It seemed he was taking charge of everything she required in order to transition to The Surface. She began to feel somewhat less anxious about her situation.

A week after her move to the Department of Temptation, Beelzebub's assistants announced that he had requested a meeting with her in the large cave typically reserved for the Ensnarement Brainstorming Team. As she waited, he sauntered in from a side entrance. Silently circling her, he looked her up and down while rubbing his chin with one hand.

"Now, about your physical transformation," he murmured, more to himself than to her.

Tarantula stood still, feeling gawked at and foolish.

"'Tis a pity you cannot shapeshift," he remarked, finally.

"You can do that?" she blurted out.

"I command a great many powers about which you know nothing," he airily replied.

Tarantula again wondered why such an experienced and admired high demon was wasting his time on someone like her. There was another uncomfortable silence which she felt compelled to break. "Then you have become a human on The Surface?" she ventured.

"Ignorant girl," he scoffed. "Why would I, Beelzebub, ever deign to 'become' a lowly human? If, by your question, you are asking whether I have changed my outward appearance to resemble that of a human, the answer is, of course, yes. My preference, however, is to possess the body of a living individual."

"Possession," she said. "Whoa."

"Whoa indeed," Beelzebub snorted. "In my six million years of tempting mankind I have wielded my power to inhabit whatever form aids me in encouraging rivalries, inciting wars, precipitating mass destruction, et cetera. Do you think Adolph Hitler was just some mere mortal? A magnificent run, that." Glancing into the distance he muttered wistfully, "I do miss that mustache."

His misty moment of nostalgia was temporary. He refocused his golden eyes on hers. "Tarantula," he intoned, "understand that hiding your true form during your time on The Surface will require sacrifice and discomfort on your part. You must inhabit your disguise at all times, for never can any being discover your true identity or purpose."

Tarantula's wings slumped as she shifted her feet and stared at the floor of the cave. "Beelzebub," she whispered, "I am afraid that Lucifer was right. Even with your expert guidance, how can I possibly pass myself off as human when I look so completely different?"

She felt a clawed finger gently lift her chin. As she raised her eyes, she was surprised to see that the high demon had the hint of a smile on his face.

"I always enjoy a challenge, my dear. For your part, you must focus, not on what makes you different, but on what you share in common with your victims. Have you not two arms, two legs, a head, and a torso? Do you not possess sensory organs similar to theirs? You have the power to reason, the ability to communicate, and have shown yourself to be inventive and clever. I never would have agreed to mentor you if I thought you were not up to this task. You must believe in yourself."

Beelzebub turned from her and clapped his hands loudly, twice. "Now let us attend to those things you do not share in common."

From a back opening in the cave marched a line of Beelzebub's private assistants, each carrying something in her arms.

"First, we must address your overall stature. You are diminutive in height compared to human teenage females. We will remedy this with a device known as high heels. Since the beginning of creation, humans have searched for ways to modify their form in order to comply with the accepted mores of their time. Remember those ridiculous fig leaves? I could engage you in a discussion regarding issues of 'beauty' and 'fashion' among mankind, especially concerning its female element, but we must move forward and, truth be told, there is no understanding it. Tempest, please."

A demon stepped out of the line, approached Tarantula, and handed her two spiky, shiny shoes. Although Tarantula had learned a great deal about human culture from the thousands of Surface Histories she had read on the insides of soul containers, she had not paid much attention to details such as fashion.

"Place these on your feet," Beelzebub ordered. "They are worn by women of many cultures as well as by some men. I have chosen alligator skin for your initial pair; I believe that will suit you."

Tarantula was pleasantly surprised to see that her pointed feet (a single toe on each foot) were readily accommodated by the tapered front of the shoes. However, after taking a few wobbling steps, she found walking difficult and the shoes painful. "These are ridiculous," she grumbled, gesturing at her feet. "I'll have to fly all the time. They hurt like crazy."

Beelzebub burst out laughing. "Ah, I knew this project would be worth my while," he chortled, rubbing his hands together. "You will learn that humans are willing to withstand terrific discomfort in their quest for attention and acceptance. The irony is simply too delicious! Don't you see? Our little torturer must endure a new world of torment in order to pursue her quest. And I am afraid you will not be doing any flying during your time on The Surface." He waved another demon forward. "Cyclone, please."

A second demon stepped out of the line carrying something tannish-brown that looked like a zippered tube with four floppy extensions. She walked up to Tarantula. "Your right foot, please."

Tarantula kicked off the annoying shoes and tried to slide her right foot and leg into one of the extensions. It was tight.

"This is known as a body suit," Beelzebub remarked as she struggled to pull the whole stretchy mess up her leg. "Human females don these to hide their bulges. You will wear this to hide your identity."

By now she was trying to get her left leg into the second tube. Confound this thing! Cyclone helped her to yank it up over her thighs. "Where's the hole for my tail?" she asked.

"Tarantula," queried Beelzebub, "in all your years in the Department of Torture, in all of the Surface Histories you have reviewed, have you ever come across a human with a tail?"

Cyclone began coiling Tarantula's tail.

"I beg your pardon," Tarantula hissed, whipping her tail out of Cyclone's grasp. The reality of the situation was beginning to dawn on her. She was being packed into what was the equivalent of an elastic sardine tin. She reached back and wound her tail into a small heap. It was one of her best features, and now she would have to hide it. She jammed it into the almost non-existent space between the suit and her back.

"A bit bulky looking, but it will have to do. Cyclone, the wings next, please."

Had he actually been serious about the no flying? This was beyond horrible. Tarantula folded her wings as close to her body as she could while Cyclone stretched the suit up and over her shoulders. With a loud snap her wings were plastered against her back.

"Right arm, please," Cyclone requested.

After a good deal of twisting and writhing, Tarantula managed to snake her arms through the two remaining tubes. Cyclone lifted the zipper that extended from her groin to her chin. She was completely encased in spandex. It was unbearable. "I'll have to remember how terrible this feels when I create my next torture narrative," she muttered.

"Not the smoothest of physiques, but satisfactory," Beelzebub stated, slowly circling Tarantula. "I believe the leather will even everything out. Sleet, Hail, please."

Two assistants walked towards her holding items made out of a dark fabric. Hail helped Tarantula into the tapered black pants, while Sleet held the jacket as she slid her arms into the sleeves. Tarantula fiddled with the buttons hidden underneath decorative zippers and metal studs. "Cool," she said, running her hands over the supple leather. "Am I ready?"

"No, Tarantula, you are not 'ready.' The devil is in the details." He slapped his thigh, pleased with his cleverness. The assistants tittered politely. "Thunder, please."

Thunder brought forward a pair of thin black socks that, once in place, served to cover the scales showing between her shoes and pant legs.

They had to be close to being finished.

"Twister, the concealer please," called out Beelzebub.

A demon came forth holding a small pot of a tan-colored substance that matched the color of Tarantula's own bronze scales.

"You must be vigilant about applying this makeup," Beelzebub warned. "Although your costume covers most of your scales, it is critical that you at all times mask what your clothing does not hide. You will need to regularly smooth this foundation on your face, neck, and hands. Beware, for it is readily removed with rubbing and exposure to liquids."

Twister began dabbing the greasy concealer on Tarantula's face. It had a sickeningly sweet smell. She closed her eye slits and tried to imagine herself back in her cozy lava pit. She felt the demon slather the stuff on her wrists and hands as well.

"Please," Tarantula begged, "I can't take much more of this. Please tell me we are finished with my transformation. I could not be more miserable."

"Just a few more touches," Beelzebub soothed. "Your ears are pointy, but I believe we can get away with that, given the wig we have chosen for you to wear."

"Wig?" Tarantula whined. "Aren't I encased enough?"

"I am afraid not," Beelzebub replied. "Typhoon, please."

A demon holding a spiky black wig cautiously sidled up next to Tarantula.

"Really going for the Goth look, aren't we?" Tarantula growled.

"Why yes, I am delighted that you recognize this particular fashion trend," Beelzebub countered. "I thought it would be most fitting given what we are working with as our baseline. Consider yourself lucky, we are holding off on any piercings for now."

Tarantula's eye slits widened but she withheld commentary. Typhoon stretched and pulled the wig to cover her frizzled hair and the tips of her ears.

"Excellent," purred Beelzebub, "I find the finished product quite satisfactory. There are a few minor tasks remaining. I recognize that you have endured much and require respite from this ordeal. After you have taken a break, my assistants will attend to your eyes, claws, and teeth."

"What?" gasped Tarantula.

"Surely you do not think your orange eyes, pointed fangs, and curved talons will make you blend right in on The Surface? My assistants will teach you how to insert contact lenses that will make your slit-shaped pupils appear round and change the color of your eyes to brown. Your teeth will be filed down, and whitening agents will be applied until the desired color is achieved. Your claws will be trimmed to a length that allows the placement of false human fingernails. You may choose any color nail polish you wish, but I suggest black, to go with the rest of your costume."

Tarantula glared at him.

"Do not look so cross. You should relax and consider this your 'spa' treatment. Now, would you like to see the result so far?"

She nodded slowly, unaccustomed to the pressure the wig exerted on her head.

"Snowstorm, the mirror please."

A twiggy demon struggled to lug a rectangular mirror over from the wall at the edge of the cave. As Tarantula peered at her reflection, she was stunned to see looking back at her a young, edgy, kickass human, albeit with fangs, claws, and orange eyes.

"I look amazing," she breathed as she smoothed down her leather jacket, "but almost everything about me is completely fake."

"Perfect," Beelzebub replied.

Up There

Tarantula didn't see much of Beelzebub after the day of her transformation. He told her only that he needed to work on arrangements and that in the meantime she would be in the care of his assistants and was to remain hidden from everyone else.

She kept herself busy by practicing putting on and taking off her disguise. The hardest part was stretching her body suit over her wings, but she figured out a way to contort her arms and back that allowed her to slip first one wing and then the other under the elastic fabric. With time, the cramps in her compressed appendages subsided. She became more adept at walking in high heels. It was devastating when her teeth were filed down and her claws clipped, but she bravely soldiered on. The contact lenses were a complete nuisance, however with repetition she became skilled at inserting and removing them, and often forgot she was wearing them at all.

Two weeks post transfer to the Department of Temptation, Beelzebub's assistants began buzzing excitedly and Tarantula guessed correctly that he was somewhere in the vicinity. He strode in as she was receiving her final teeth bleaching treatment.

"Everything is in order," he announced. He peered into her face. "Ah, I see that you have made progress. Your eyes are particularly convincing."

"Are we going to The Surface? You haven't told me anything, I won't know what to do," she mumbled through the thick white paste.

"There will be ample time to discuss details, Tarantula. You must understand that most of what you will need to learn will occur 'on the job' as they say."

Wait, what? Wasn't she going to be given a Surface Manual of some sort? Get a few lessons on how to act human? Was he going to just throw her up there and make her fend for herself? Sure, she had been reading Surface Histories for decades, but this was the real thing. She felt an awful churning sensation inside of her belly. This must be anxiety, she thought grimly. She had induced it in countless souls back in Lava Pit 103. Now she was getting a taste of her own medicine.

Beelzebub sensed her fear. "Do not fret, Tarantula," he said quietly. "This will be your first time on The Surface, but I have journeyed there countless times. I will not abandon you. In fact, I will be your family. Your uncle, to be precise."

She spat out the nasty paste, rinsed her mouth with acid, and asked, "Will you be wearing a disguise as well?"

Beelzebub laughed. "And be as morbidly uncomfortable as you are? Certainly not. I have identified just the right human to possess, and in his body, I will easily be able to provide us with the shelter, resources, and back story we require over the course of our stay."

Our stay. Beelzebub would be remaining on The Surface with her. That was a huge relief. The roiling in her gut ratcheted down a notch. "What is our story? Where are we going? Tell me more," she begged.

"In good time. All is prepared. Are you ready?"

Tarantula took in a deep breath. She thought about how skilled she was now with her disguise. There was nothing more to be learned here. She looked around the cavern. She would miss the flickering firelight, the heat and smoke, the soft rumble of flowing lava in the background. But the time had come for her next adventure.

"I am ready," she replied in a steady voice.

Beelzebub scrutinized her briefly. "You will require the use of your wings. Remove your costume, place your belongings in this leather backpack, and meet me at the conveyor."

In a whirl, he was gone.

Tarantula excitedly wiped off her makeup, popped out her contact lenses, and slipped off her shoes, socks, leather clothing, bodysuit and wig. It felt glorious to expand her wings to their full length and to lash her tail. She flew around the cave for a bit to stretch her unused muscles.

Thunder and Lightning helped her to pack her outfit and added to the bag contact lens supplies, three containers of concealer, a manicure set complete with nail polish and remover, a toothbrush with extra tooth whitener, and an inflatable stand for her wig.

"You are very brave," whispered Thunder.

"We are all rooting for you," added Lightning as she patted Tarantula lightly on the shoulder.

"I wouldn't go up there in a million years," someone hissed from outside of the cave.

Beelzebub was waiting for her by the conveyor. As the door slid open and they stepped inside, he ignored the usual indicator buttons and fitted a delicate silver key into a hole high up on the control panel. He noticed her curious glance.

"Only a select few have access to The Surface. With this key, the conveyor will take us nearly all the way up through The Crust. There is a tunnel that connects the furthermost conveyor platform to the Kidd Creek Mine in Ontario. It is the deepest base metal mine on earth."

"Is that where we're going, to Canada?" She was trying hard to be patient but had so many questions for him.

"Our final destination is the United States. We have quite a bit of flying to do."

"Why …."

Beelzebub stopped her with a glare. "Tarantula, all will be made known to you soon. Note that I am accustomed to traveling alone. I request that you speak no more until we have completed our journey."

They rocketed up through the earth in silence.

They stepped out of the conveyor into a dark tunnel.

"It is good to be back," Beelzebub mused. "Allow me a moment."

Tarantula observed for the first time that he had brought no belongings with him. He took a few steps away from her, shuddered violently, and disappeared.

What? Where had he gone? Great goblins, was he planning on leaving her in a cave somewhere in Canada, expecting she would get to wherever she was going on her own? She was about to yell his name when she was distracted by an annoying buzzing in her ear. A black fly was circling her head. What was a fly doing in a mine shaft deep in the earth? She tried to swat it away, but it evaded her blow and landed on her nose. Yellow eyes stared angrily into hers.

Beelzebub.

The fly took off down a stretch of tunnel. She secured her backpack between her wings, lifted into the air, and sped after him. Her short wingspan and compact body allowed her to easily maneuver through the curving passageway. Eventually they made a sharp turn and she could tell that they were flying up, far up. The air was changing; it felt cooler, thinner. Suddenly they burst from the entrance of the mine into the night.

Her eyes slowly adjusted to the ambient light which came mostly from the stars overhead. How beautiful they were! She had heard about stars of course, but they were more numerous and brilliant than she had expected. As she continued to look around, that first positive impression of The Surface faded away. Looming in front of her were four large, ugly metal buildings. The land was rocky, pitted, and desolate. Had she travelled all this way only to learn that The Surface looked no different than some of the bleaker areas in Hell? Where were the houses, neighborhoods, and people she had seen in the Surface Histories? And would that infernal buzzing ever stop?

Beelzebub landed on her nose again and this time gave her a painful bite. She resisted the urge to smack him, recognizing that this was a reprimand for being so distracted. She needed to keep her focus on him, and on their journey ahead. As he darted into the sky she obediently followed.

In a southern direction they traveled, over Canada, into the United States, and down the East Coast. Never had she been asked to fly so far; she was relieved to find that her wings were powerful and steady. She understood that this would be the last time she would be allowed to use them for quite a while, so she savored the feel of the air rushing over them and the lift from surrounding currents.

They flew rapidly through the night. There were countless things to see, hear, and smell, but she reminded herself there would be plenty of time to explore and kept her attention riveted on the tiny insect zooming forward. As the first notes of birdsong began to filter up from far below, Beelzebub led her sharply downward. Now she began identifying the clusters of streets, houses, and cars that she recognized as neighborhoods. There were no humans about, but she reminded herself that they required sleep and were not typically active during the pre-dawn hours. Beelzebub descended quickly now, circling once, twice, and landing on the doormat of a darkened house with white shutters that was situated at the end of a cul-de-sac. Untrimmed branches from large bushes in the yard shrouded the entrance. Tarantula touched down, exhausted, on the cement stairs that led up to the front door.

Beelzebub flew up and perched on the doorbell button. He vibrated his wings to create the irritating humming noise. Tarantula watched him expectantly. Moments later, he took off, made two tight circles, landed on the doorbell again, and produced a particularly prolonged buzz. Tarantula understood at last, climbed the steps, and pushed the button.

It took four rings before someone came to the door. She saw a light come on inside the house, and then heard a fumbling, first with the lock, and then with the security chain. The door swung open to reveal a bleary-eyed human male in rumpled striped pajamas, with hair sticking out from his head. He glared down at Tarantula.

"What the devil …," he said, but before he could finish his sentence, Beelzebub flew straight up his nose.

Fitting In

The man abruptly stopped speaking and stared blankly ahead. Seconds ticked by. Suddenly a glint came into his eyes, and he turned his gaze on Tarantula.

"It took you long enough," he snapped.

"E-excuse me?" she stammered.

"To ring the doorbell, for Hell's sake. Do not just stand there, come in."

The man opened the door wider, and Tarantula stumbled over the threshold. The house was dark and had an odd smell. She slowly backed away from him as he shut and locked the door.

"Well, what do you think?" he asked, sweeping his arm around the small foyer.

"Beelzebub, is that you?" she whispered.

"Uncle B to you."

The man lifted his shaggy eyebrows, tilted his head and began nodding. The loose skin under his chin waggled back and forth. This was going to take some getting used to.

"Why did you choose this body and this place?"

"There were many factors to take into account for our needs, Tarantula. I have been tracking Bernard Smith for some time now, for a variety of reasons. He is a self-serving, egotistical misanthrope who never married or had any offspring. After swindling his siblings out of their family fortune and alienating the remainder of his relatives, he chose to live in seclusion in the outskirts of this city. He is virtually unknown to the community. Although he chooses to live modestly, his finances are ample. At age forty-eight, it is plausible that he would have an eighteen-year-old niece come live with him after the tragic death of her parents."

"And I am that eighteen-year-old niece," she said, catching on. "Where exactly is this city?"

"We are in Deadham, North Carolina. Again, many elements went into the decision-making concerning where you should begin the Temptation Project. It is in our best interest to place you in an environment that is conducive to the greatest chance of success. There are two large universities in the area filled with adolescents upon whom you might prey. In addition, the Deadham

Public School system currently has nine middle schools and eleven high schools and there are a number of private schools as well. Then there were concerns regarding climate."

"Climate," she repeated.

"Yes, Tarantula, clearly you have no idea how complex the challenges are of integrating a demon into human society. How do you find the temperature in North Carolina so far?"

Tarantula considered his question. "It's a little chilly, but I can stand it. It will be better when I am wearing my body suit and leather."

"You are comfortable because it is early July and the current ambient temperature is ninety-eight degrees Fahrenheit. I timed our arrival to coincide with a heat wave. It will take a while for you to become adjusted to living on The Surface, and you may never truly feel acclimated here. I could have chosen a warmer climate, and targeted, say, Florida, but keep in mind that you are required to wear clothing that will hide your scales to the greatest extent possible. We do not want your long sleeves and pants to look completely out of place. North Carolina seemed a reasonable compromise. It does snow here occasionally in the winter. We will face that situation when it arises."

Snow? As in crystallized water? She hadn't considered the possibility that someday she might have to be in contact with that repulsive substance. Just the thought of handling a glass filled with ice cubes made her shudder.

"Speaking of adjusting," Beelzebub continued, "there is something I must attend to immediately. It is almost daybreak."

The man walked into the room to the left of the front door and began lowering the blinds and pulling the curtains closed. Then he crossed the foyer and entered the room to the right and repeated his actions. She listened to his footsteps as he made his way around the rest of the house. While he was gone, she wandered into the room on the left. There was a saggy tan couch beneath the windows that faced the front yard. Two armchairs with faded tan and maroon stripe upholstery were angled towards one another a few feet from the opposite wall. Between the couch and chairs sat an oval glass coffee table scattered with newspapers that only partially hid the congealed foodstuffs on its surface. A frayed red and green braided rug covered the floor. On the far wall hung a rectangular TV. This must be the living room. It didn't bode well for the décor in the rest of the house.

"It would be prudent to keep the blinds and curtains closed at all times," Beelzebub said, reentering the room. "The glare of the sun will initially be disagreeable to you, although your contact lenses will lessen your discomfort somewhat. In addition, privacy is paramount. We do not want our neighbors asking questions or noticing anything unusual. You must be vigilant about this. I see you have already viewed the living room. Would you like a tour of the rest of the house?"

Without waiting for an answer, he turned and headed towards the room to the right of the foyer.

"You have a bald spot, you know," she said, trailing after him. "You're also a little flabby around the middle. We're going to have to work on your diet and exercise."

Beelzebub stopped walking. Slowly he turned to face her. There was a tense moment of silence. Then, as if on cue, they both burst out laughing.

"The things I do to honor Lucifer," he said, wiping his eyes with the back of his hand. "These eyebrows, it is like trying to see through a thicket. And the nose hairs are practically touching my upper lip. Does this human not believe in personal hygiene? Ah well. This is the dining room. You, of course, will have no need of either the dining room or the kitchen. But while I inhabit this body, I must nourish it."

She took in the mahogany table marred by numerous dents and scratches in the center of the room. It was surrounded by eight chairs upholstered in an unattractive multicolored velvety fabric. A dusty chandelier hung above it. Three out of its six light bulbs were missing. A threadbare oriental rug covered the hardwood floor.

They walked through an arched opening in the back of the dining room into the kitchen. The appliances and cabinets were all a matching shade of avocado green. A round white table with two chairs sat in one corner. Hovering protectively over the table was a pink glass light fixture suspended from the ceiling. The sink was piled high with dirty dishes.

In the center of house was a staircase that led to the second floor. At the top of the steps, Beelzebub gestured to the two doors that opened off of the landing. "This door leads to your bedroom and en suite bathroom. The other is to my bedroom and bathroom. Although you have no physical requirement for sleep, it is suitable for you to have quarters of your own. Unfortunately, acid baths are strictly prohibited here. Once, during a prolonged stay on The Surface, I was so desperate for a proper cleansing that I secured the appropriate acid from a chemical company. Let me warn you that items crafted by humans are nothing of the quality that we enjoy in

Hell. Needless to say, the tub in which I placed the acid dissolved immediately, along with the pipes and the flooring beneath, and the whole mess fell into the basement of the structure I was inhabiting. It was an extremely difficult situation to explain. I do not plan on repeating that error again. I have found that steaming hot water, with forceful pressure, is a poor but acceptable substitute. We will engage a plumber if your shower is not satisfactory."

She said nothing. There was so much to absorb. She opened her door and peered into her room. There were two windows facing the street, a queen-sized bed covered with an orange and brown plaid quilt, a drab wooden nightstand with a lamp on it, and a tilted dresser with four drawers. Everything was blanketed with a layer of dust. She couldn't bear to look at the bathroom yet. At least she would have some privacy. They walked back down the stairs and sat at the table in the dining room.

"Now," Beelzebub said, leaning back in his chair and folding his hands across his ample belly.

It was impossible to believe that the baggy old man seated across the table from her was the elegant demon she had first encountered in the Hall of Lucifer. She was struggling to take him seriously, especially in those pajamas.

"What is your strategy regarding the Temptation Project?" he asked.

She was completely flustered by his question. So much of her energy had been devoted to looking like a human and getting to The Surface that she hadn't thought at all about what she would do once she got here.

"Um, well," she stammered, "I'm going to tempt human teenagers."

"And how, exactly, do you propose to execute that?" he pressed.

"Beelzebub, honestly, I haven't really thought about my next steps," she admitted.

"I am now Uncle B to you," he admonished. "You must never utter the name Beelzebub up here." He softened his tone and added, "I have pondered this matter and have some suggestions for you."

She leaned forward, eager to hear his insights.

"First, at no time can you forget who and what you are. You will eventually become comfortable in the company of humans but remember that you are not one of them. Be diligent about your disguise, and remove it only when you are absolutely sure no human will see you."

He paused for emphasis, and then continued.

"You will need to hide the fact that you neither sleep nor eat. It is very easy, although tedious, to pretend to sleep when that is called for. Eating is more complicated. You can chew and swallow small amounts, but be aware that you have no capacity to digest what you ingest. Therefore, if you choose to eat or drink, you must see to it that you remove what you have swallowed at some point."

"How do I do that?" she wondered aloud.

"The easiest way is to find the nearest lavatory and induce vomiting."

I'm never doing that, Tarantula thought.

"What do you plan on doing about your breath?" Beelzebub asked.

"Why, is it bad? Do I need a mint?" she quipped.

"This is not a game, Tarantula," he said sternly. "I am expecting you to know at least the basics about the human race, and certainly hope that you are aware that they do not spit fire when they are angered."

Oh. She had not taken into account that detail.

"The obvious way to address this issue is to control your anger. But if you truly plan to masquerade as a human teenager, I believe emotional outbursts will be a necessary part of that charade. You might consider chewing ice as a precaution."

Chewing ice? That was not going to happen either. "But won't that look unusual to humans?"

"My dear, we have done our best regarding your outward appearance. But even given the superb skills of my assistants, you must accept that you look … well, a bit odd. There will be aspects of your story, character, and life that will raise questions among humans. Be clever, be resourceful, and never give yourself away. I am counting on you for this."

She nodded, aware that any failure on her part would place both her existence and Beelzebub's reputation in jeopardy. He was taking a risk to assist her.

"My understanding is that you plan to use your time on The Surface to tempt humans, with the ultimate goal of speeding their demise and increasing our numbers in Hell. Am I correct in this assumption?"

She nodded.

"Then use your wits. Harness the creativity and energy you demonstrated when you developed the Adolescent Torture Area. Set a reasonable goal for yourself. I suggest aiming for the endpoint of welcoming six new souls to Hell by the end of our six-month trial period. I believe that number will adequately impress Lucifer."

Six souls. That didn't sound too difficult. She nodded again.

"Remember, I am your uncle, Bernard Smith. You will refer to me as Uncle B. I am retired from a job in finance. Your father was my brother. Your parents recently died in a car crash, and you are now my ward. Your name is Tarantula Smith. You are eighteen. The rest of the details you can invent as needed, as long as you are consistent. To that effect, sharing less information with others means less remembering for you. Be vague, it will serve you well."

She repeated this information to herself.

"Will I go to school?" she asked.

"Attending an educational institution would be complicated, as there are many subjects that you would be required to master in too little time. We shall say that you are preparing to sit for the General Education Development tests, better known as getting your GED, in lieu of completing high school.

"But if I'm not going to school, how will I hunt my prey?"

"Well, Tarantula," Beelzebub slowly replied, "I will make the recommendation to you that I believe many human parents suggest to their adolescent offspring." His lips curved into self-satisfied smirk. "Go out and get a job."

The Job

As the sun rose higher in the sky, Tarantula became increasingly uncomfortable with the brightness of her surroundings. She eventually retreated to the basement. There was not much down there besides a furnace, hot water heater, and a few pieces of broken furniture. It smelled of damp cement and mildew. Because it was chillier there, she had dressed in her human costume. Even the wig felt good, as it provided additional warmth.

While pacing back and forth in an effort to decrease her shivering, she considered making a fire with her breath. Much of the old furniture was made of wood. She decided against it, not wanting to burn the house down during her first morning on The Surface.

It had been embarrassing last night when Beelzebub put her on the spot regarding how she would implement the Temptation Project. Now the enormity of her responsibilities weighed on her. There was no need for panic yet. She remembered how intimidating it was at first to set up the Adolescent Torture Area. The whole enterprise seemed overwhelming. But after she broke down the colossal challenge into smaller goals, it became much more manageable. She would use the same technique with the Temptation Project.

Let's see. Goal number one would have to be the successful delivery of adolescent souls to Lucifer. If she didn't accomplish this, her very existence remained at risk. Beelzebub had said something to Lucifer about banishing her to the Department of Lava Maintenance, but she knew the punishment for failure could be fatal. Last night, Beelzebub had suggested six souls in six months. That sounded achievable.

The second goal should be the thing both Beelzebub and Lucifer had warned about. Her identity must remain absolutely secret. No human could ever learn what she really was. This meant she had to be ever mindful about maintaining her disguise. If she was careless and let her guard down even for a moment, that would be the end of the Temptation Project and probably her as well.

The third and final goal was what worried her the most. She must manage her own dark secret. If she couldn't eradicate the impulse to feel sympathy for her victims, she had to learn to control it. It could not be allowed to influence her work again. Beelzebub must never know.

She heard the front door open and close. Someone had entered the house. Heavy footsteps thudded down the wooden stairs to the basement.

"I thought I might find you down here," Beelzebub said.

"Where have you been?"

"There are many inconveniences that must be endured while possessing a human body. One must feed it, permit it to sleep, keep it out of harm's way, and maintain its health. I required some things from the store."

She was curious. "What did you need?"

"If you must know, we were out of toilet paper."

Tarantula barked out a laugh. "Maybe having to wear a disguise isn't so bad after all, considering the alternative."

"Quite possibly," Beelzebub acknowledged. "In any event, I made some purchases for you." He reached into the bag he was holding and brought out a pair of black plastic sunglasses. "Not the most fashionable, as they are from the pharmacy, but they should provide you with some relief from the glare until you adjust."

Tarantula took them from him and put them on. "Much better, thank you," she said, flashing him a grateful glance over the dark lenses.

He fished around in the bag again, pulled out two objects, and handed them to her.

"Cigarettes and a lighter?" she said, surprised. "Not what I would expect from my nurturing Uncle B."

He ignored her sarcasm. "I suspect in time you may get homesick, Tarantula. I find when I tire of The Surface and long for the comforts of Hell, the flame of the lighter and a deep inhalation of hot smoke lift my spirits. But you make an important point: it is illegal for a human under the age of twenty-one to purchase tobacco products, and it would be prudent for you not to use these around adults. There is a stigma associated with cigarette smoking that can be both positive and negative, so choose your environments wisely. It goes without saying that the health risks are not an issue for you."

He folded up the bag. "One more thing," he said. "I noticed a 'Help Wanted' sign in the window of the pharmacy."

Tarantula stiffened. Employment. This was all happening so fast.

Beelzebub paused for a moment to allow her to process this information.

"I think this may be the perfect opportunity for you," he continued matter-of-factly. "First, the pharmacy is within walking distance, so we would not have to bother with the intricacies of obtaining a car, teaching you how to drive, and procuring your driver's license. Second, the pharmacy sells a wide variety of necessities, which means people from different walks of life will frequent it. You would be exposed to humans of assorted ages and backgrounds and will learn about their requirements. This knowledge will improve your insight into human society. Third, the store is on the edge of the Earl University undergraduate campus. Adolescent students will be regular customers."

Tarantula considered his points. Beelzebub, she noted, could be quite persuasive.

"What do I have to do?" she sighed.

"I suggest you simply walk down to the store today and inquire about the position."

He turned and trudged back up the stairs. From the top step he called down, "Remember, use your wits."

Tarantula remained in the basement until the cold seeped under her scales and she could no longer stand the trembling. She tried a few cigarettes and found they provided some temporary warmth and comfort. The ash she flicked onto the cement floor brought back fond memories of Hell. Slowly she climbed the stairs. With her new sunglasses in place, she could tolerate the glare of the light inside the house. But when she cracked the front door open in an attempt to step outside, the sunlight was blinding. Better to wait until nightfall. She found Beelzebub sitting at the kitchen table reading a newspaper.

"Now this is a homey scene," she sniffed.

"I am trying to keep up with my progress in the Middle East," he sighed, setting the paper aside. Looking up at Tarantula, he said, "On the dining room table you will find a cellular telephone, a charger, and the instructions for their use. The phone will assist you in gathering information and interacting socially. Carry this device with you at all times and pay it an absurd amount of attention. Otherwise, humans will become suspicious of you. I warn you to avoid the games; they are devilishly distracting. I have also left you a credit card with the name Tarantula Smith imprinted on it. Charge whatever purchases you believe are vital to the success of the Temptation Project. Your copy of the house key is there as well."

She went into the dining room to examine the cell phone, credit card, and key. She spent the remainder of the daylight hours up in her room figuring out how to use her phone. It was astonishing how much she was able to learn about humans in such a short period of time. This jewel would be the guidebook to The Surface she had hoped to receive.

At dusk, she mustered her courage, picked up her backpack full of supplies, and marched into her bathroom. It wasn't too awful. Facing her reflection in the mirror above the sink, she took off her sunglasses, inserted her contact lenses, adjusted her wig, and applied makeup to her face, neck, and hands. Then she stomped down the stairs and approached the front door. After turning the lock and removing the chain, she slowly cracked it open. The sun had almost set; the glare from the streetlights was tolerable. She took a tentative step outside.

Using the map function on her phone, she set off to find the pharmacy. The neighborhood was deserted except for a tall girl walking a woolly dog on the opposite side of the street.

Now that she wasn't streaking through the night in mad pursuit of Beelzebub, she could focus on her surroundings. There were so many sensations to experience all at once. A warm breeze passed over her face; the air was remarkably free of ash. Its scent, a mixture of car exhaust, cut grass, flowers, and dozens of other sources she had read about, was so different from the sulfurous tang of Hell. Her ears rang with the steady drone of crickets and frogs, occasionally punctuated by a car horn or the distant call of a human voice. So, this was a summer evening. Her eyes traveled over houses, lawns, roads, motorized vehicles, and power lines, up to wispy clouds that were turning into streaks of red and orange in the darkening sky.

Her high heels clicked rhythmically as she made her way down sidewalks and across streets to the pharmacy. On the front window of the store was taped a sign that read, "Cashier Wanted, Apply Within." Hesitating, she gazed across the busy intersection at the entrance to the Earl University undergraduate campus. Grassy hills rolled back from the low stone wall that marked the campus boundary. Through lush trees she made out stately brick buildings. Students in the distance walked in twos and threes, chatting and holding books. She licked her lips.

The door of the pharmacy swung open. As an old human woman slowly exited, she slipped inside. Immediately she was bombarded by color, light, and sound. Everywhere she turned there were hundreds of brightly colored objects for sale in cluttered freestanding displays, jam-packed shelves along the aisles, and racks against the walls. Music oozed out of two speakers mounted near the ceiling. She turned and observed a young woman standing in the corner of the room surrounded by a fortress of candy and gum. That was most likely the cashier.

Tarantula wandered down the nearest aisle. Did humans really need all of this stuff? It was inconceivable. She had read that pharmacies supplied medicines, but this place seemed to sell everything. Would she be able to handle a job here? She picked up a package of sanitary napkins. Ah, yes, feminine hygiene products. Human menstruation, Mother Nature's very own torture narrative. She felt a surge of relief knowing this was one human thing she personally did not have to deal with. Her eyes drifted over to a stack of purple boxes that had something about yeast infections printed on them.

"May I help you?" a voice said behind her.

She froze. A human was talking to her. This was it, her first live human interaction. She carefully placed the bag of sanitary napkins back on the shelf and turned around. A middle-aged man with thin white hair and dark circles under his eyes was watching her with what might be suspicion. She was positive she'd put her contacts in. Had her makeup smeared? Were her scales showing?

"I ... I was just comparing prices," she stammered uncomfortably.

The man took a few moments to look her up and down. He seemed particularly wary of her studded jacket. "I've not seen you in the store before, so I wanted to make sure you didn't need assistance," he said tersely.

In order to become the superb torture narrative creator that she was, Tarantula had to first develop a keen insight into her victims' thoughts and perceptions. Her eye slits opened a fraction wider. This human was judging her. It seemed Beelzebub did her no favors by having his assistants dress her in black leather and spiky alligator heels. She steadied herself and responded as cheerfully as she could.

"Actually, I am here to apply for the cashier job."

The man drew back and pursed his lips. "The position," he said, "you are interested in the cashier position."

"Yes," she replied firmly.

"Well, I am the person you would speak to about that, but it's late and I was about to leave for home."

"You'll find me a hard worker," she pressed, "and a quick learner. For example, I've noticed that you carry seven brands of sanitary napkins with ten levels of absorption and that the price differential between brands ranges from two cents to twenty-six cents per napkin."

"Very impressive," he murmured. "I do need the help. How soon would you be able to start?"

"Immediately," Tarantula said.

The man hesitated, shook his head, and said, "Follow me."

He turned and walked briskly to the back of the store. She followed him through a door marked "Employees Only." They continued along a narrow corridor, then swerved into a room on the left. The small office was illuminated by a dim light bulb that hung from a wire in the middle of the ceiling. Brown plywood paneling on the walls made the room dingy and dark. A desk in the center of the office was laden with stacks of paper. The worn brown carpeting needed a good vacuuming.

The man rounded the desk and lowered himself into a swivel chair. He rubbed his eyes. "Have a seat," he said, gesturing to a metal folding chair that was in the back corner. "I'm Mr. Hanson. Your name is?"

She dragged the chair closer to the desk and perched uncomfortably on its cold surface. "Tarantula Smith," she replied, trying to make her voice sound relaxed.

Mr. Hanson looked perturbed. "Tarantula like the spider?"

She hated it when her name was mispronounced. "Tarantula like the dance, the Tarantella. The accent is on the third syllable, Tar-an-TOO-la."

"Right," he said uneasily. "Now then, do you have any experience working in a pharmacy?"

"No," she said slowly. "But ...."

"Ever work in a store?"

"No," she admitted, "But ...."

"If you have no experience, why on earth would I hire you?" he asked testily.

Why on earth indeed. Come on, Tarantula, you can do this.

"Because I do have experience," she answered. "I have a great deal of experience in customer service. I always ensure that my customers get what they deserve." Her lips curled slightly at the thought. "In fact, I recently won a service award."

That seemed to reassure him a bit.

"Would you be able to provide a reference?"

Tarantula thought of Beelzebub. If he could incite world wars, she didn't think acting as a reference would be beyond his capabilities. "Of course," she said with a smile. She tried showing her teeth a little.

The man leaned back in his seat and picked up a pen from the desk. He flicked it to and fro between his fingers. It was irritating.

"Can you work a cash register?"

"I am confident I can master it in no time."

Still, he hesitated. He kept glancing at her wig. Secretly, he was put off by the whole black leather thing. She was tiny; without those shoes, she would be, what, four feet tall at most? And that skin, what was with all the makeup? How old was she, anyway?

"How old are you?" he asked. "Are you in school?"

"I am eighteen," she replied. "I live with my uncle in town. I just moved here. I am studying to get my GED."

There was a long pause. She felt the interview wasn't going in the direction she wanted. What had Beelzebub advised her? Ah, yes, to use her wits.

The man moved around uncomfortably in his chair and fidgeted with the pen some more.

"I'm sorry," he began, "but I don't think …."

Tarantula dropped her head into her hands and let out a moan. "The truth is," she said in a shaky voice, "my parents were recently killed in a car accident. After the lawyer helped me to sell our home and settle our debts, I had only enough money left to pay for their funerals. I don't know what I would have done if my uncle, Mr. Smith, hadn't taken me in. I really need this job." Raising her head slightly, she sniffed a few times and brushed away an imaginary tear. "I am smart, hard-working, and will be someone you can count on."

She could tell the man across the desk was moved. Stupid gullible human.

"Well," he choked out, "I am sorry for your loss. I do need the help. The college students I normally employ are away for the summer and I've been pulling double shifts. I could use a break. What hours can you work? We're open twenty-four hours a day, seven days a week."

She looked up at him with her eyebrows lifted so as to appear more pathetic. "I prefer nights," she said, still using the weepy tone. "And I won't need any time off."

He seemed to perk up a little when she said this.

"Fine, let's start you on the graveyard shift, from 11 p.m. until 7 a.m. We'll see how it goes. Fill out this paperwork and bring it with you when you start tomorrow night at 11."

The graveyard shift. She liked the sound of that.

A Change of Plan

In her mind, she referred to Mr. Hanson as Mr. Handsome. That way, every time she thought about or talked to him, she could have her own private laugh. After exiting his office with the paperwork, Tarantula spent the next hour roaming up and down the aisles absorbing every detail about the merchandise. This wasn't going to be as complicated as she had initially thought.

While she was there, she observed the people coming into the pharmacy. No one paid any attention to her, which was reassuring; she must not look that strange. The Earl University students interested her the most. Their dress was referred to as "preppy" on the internet sites she had visited earlier that day. Her wardrobe would require broadening if she was going to fit in. Let's see. Shorts were out because of her scales, but a few pairs of jeans would do the trick. Shirts would be more complicated because they had to be long-sleeved and high-necked. She could use scarves to cover her scaly throat, but that would involve learning how to tie them. She shivered in the air-conditioned store. Beelzebub was right; she was never going to feel warm on The Surface.

A rack of magazines caught her eye. She picked up the latest edition of *Seventeen* and flipped through it, digesting the contents of each page with a momentary glance. It was truly unbelievable, the silly things humans spent their time thinking about. She looked over *People Magazine* and *Vogue* in seconds as well. Shaking her head, she put the magazines back in the rack. That was about all the popular culture she could stand for one evening.

She noticed that almost every adolescent and adult female in the store had some degree of paint on her face. The magazines confirmed her suspicion that, along with the foundation she wore, additional makeup was necessary to make her disguise more convincing. She circled around to the cosmetics area and zeroed in on a brand that was advertised in *Seventeen*. Eyeliner, mascara, blush, and lipstick seemed like a decent start.

As she stood in the checkout line, she watched how the cashier manipulated the register. It seemed easy enough; swipe a credit card or take the cash and put it in the drawer. The machine even calculated the amount of change that was due back. When it was her turn to pay, she offered the girl the credit card Beelzebub had provided. It was accepted without a hitch. When the cashier handed back the card with a small piece of paper and a pen for her signature, she illegibly scribbled the words "Demon from Hell" just for fun.

On the walk back to the house, her cul-de-sac was quiet. It wasn't much of a happening neighborhood, which was probably one of the reasons why Beelzebub had selected it. As she was unlocking her front door, out of the corner of her eye she glimpsed the tall girl she had seen earlier that evening emerging from the house across the street. Tarantula slid around the door and shut it quickly behind her.

The house was dark, and the only sound was the hum of various appliances. She walked in and put her package down on the dining room table. Through the archway she spied the intermittent red glow of a cigarette tip in the kitchen.

"How did it go?" asked Beelzebub as she entered.

He was seated at the white Formica kitchen table, tipped back in one of the green chairs. Forming his mouth into an O, he blew out a wreath of smoke that took the shape of a dragon before dissipating into the air.

"I got the job," she said, pulling out the chair across from his and sitting down. "I need you to serve as my reference."

Beelzebub swung his chair forward so that all four legs rested on the floor. He placed his elbows on the table and said, "Well done, Tarantula. It would be an honor." Tapping his chin with an index finger, he added, "How shall I refer to your previous place of employment? Torturers R Us? Perhaps PainMart?"

"This is serious. Do not mess this up for me," Tarantula groaned.

"My dear, I would not think of it," he replied, waving around the cigarette. "One must keep one's sense of humor among these humans, remember that." He inhaled deeply from the cigarette and blew another smoke ring, this one in the shape of a striking cobra.

"You're going to have to teach me how to do that," she murmured as she watched a tiny flame flicker from the cobra's open mouth before it melted away. "How's it going in the Middle East?"

"Not well, not well at all." Beelzebub's saggy face took on a look of concern. "Tarantula, there is something urgent I must discuss with you."

She was wary of his sudden change in tone.

"I know that Lucifer is willing to give you six months on The Surface to prove the Temptation Project has merit. But I simply cannot remain in this body for that length of time." He reached for the cracked coffee cup sitting on the table and stubbed out his cigarette. "I am needed in a variety of pressing situations. The American president has become much too friendly with the leader of Russia and this cannot be allowed to progress. There is confrontation in Syria that must be inflamed. This body," he waved his arm irritably across his torso, "is cumbersome and does not allow me the flexibility to go where and when I am needed. But if I exit it now, you will no longer have a place to live or a credible backstory."

"So what are you saying?" she asked cautiously.

"The only solution is to shorten the duration of the Temptation Project."

Shorten the Temptation Project? Vipers vexations, she was just getting started.

"How short?"

He held her gaze for a moment, and then replied, "One month."

A narrow tongue of flame burst from her mouth and set fire to the dishrag that was draped over the handle of the oven door.

"A month?" she yelled. "How am I supposed to get anything done in a month?"

Beelzebub calmly looked over at the pile of ash on the floor. "Temper, temper. I do not want to have to go looking for another house. I am aware that this is a rather large shift in our time frame."

"Rather large?" she shrieked. "What you're asking me to do is impossible!"

Another jet of flame flashed across the room and incinerated the potholder that had been hanging on a hook on the wall a moment before.

"That is quite enough, Tarantula," Beelzebub warned in a low voice.

Even though he was in that ugly, decrepit body, she could still feel his power and presence, and knew she'd better not push her point too far.

"This is not a discussion, this is the plan," he continued firmly. "We will remain in this house for one month. Twenty-nine days to be precise, as this is the end of the first day. Within this period of time, you will use your skills to tempt six mortals to make choices that will damn them to Lucifer's domain."

Tarantula leaned over the table and buried her face in her arms. Maybe her crying routine would work on Beelzebub as well as it had on Mr. Handsome.

"Why would you set me up to fail, Uncle B?" she moaned.

He smiled at her cleverly-timed use of his new name. "Think of it as an intellectual challenge," he said in a lighter manner. "You don't really want to be a mindless worker in that dreary drug store for six months, do you? As you well know, adolescent friendships can be easily and quickly established. I believe you will find this pace more to your liking once you have identified your targets and are moving ahead with your scheme."

"One month," she muttered, lifting her head. "But there is so much to do. I don't even have the right clothes."

"Ah, at least I can help you with that issue," Beelzebub replied, eager to change the subject. "My assistants anticipated that once you were settled in, your wardrobe would require tweaking. You will find your bedroom stocked with items to supplement your disguise. If their choices are not to your liking, feel free to use the credit card I gave you to purchase whatever you would like."

New clothes without having to go shopping? That was something. There was no use in moping around Beelzebub. They both knew she had to play by his rules. Slowly she rose from the table. Well, if she was going to spend her time around teenagers, she might as well get some practice acting like one.

Tarantula lunged towards Beelzebub and threw her arms around his neck. After rubbing her cheek against his beard stubble and depositing a coating of foundation there, she sprang backwards and shouted, "Thanks, Uncle B, you're the best!" Leaving him stunned, she ran from the kitchen and bounded up the stairs to her bedroom.

Prospect Number One

At 10:20 the next evening, Tarantula was on her way back to the pharmacy. Beelzebub's assistants had done a fine job of adding to her wardrobe. The items were still mostly black, but they had branched out by selecting a few accessories in muted colors. There was nothing flowery or ruffled, she was grateful to note. Most importantly, her new clothes looked like they would keep her warm. She was thrilled to find in her closet a pair of boots that looked considerably more comfortable than the alligator high heels she had been enduring. She tossed the stilettos into the garbage can in the kitchen on her way out of the house.

She had chosen black jeans, a black turtleneck, and a pale yellow sweater to wear on her first night of work. On her feet were the platform boots that gave her additional height without pitching her body forward at a forty-five degree angle. Beelzebub was right, human fashion was ludicrous. She laughed at herself for the absurd amount of time she had spent applying her new makeup.

As she drew nearer to the store, she felt a wave of discomfort somewhere in her midsection. She paused on the sidewalk. During the day she had spent time searching the Internet for information about "first day on the job" so that she would know how to behave this evening. Surely this could not be what humans referred to as a case of nerves? Ridiculous. She went behind a tall hedge and let out a good cough, which made her feel a little better. The circle of scorched lawn she left behind was barely noticeable. She continued her walk to the pharmacy.

After patting her wig and pulling down her sweater one final time, she entered the store. She walked straight to the back, through the "Employees Only" door, and down the corridor to the office she had visited the previous night. The door was ajar, casting a rectangle of light on the floor of the hallway. She knocked tentatively on the doorframe.

"Come in," a harried voice snapped.

"I'm sorry to trouble you, Mr. Hanson, but I am here for my first night of work," she said in a soft voice.

He looked up, disoriented. "What? Oh, come in. You're early."

"Yes," she said. "You will find that I am an employee who is never late."

"That's good to hear," he grumbled.

Putting down the papers he had been reviewing, he ran a hand through his sparse hair and studied her for a moment. She still looked mighty peculiar but was more presentable tonight without all that black leather. He hoped she would not scare away the customers.

Pushing his chair back from the desk and standing, he said, "Come with me, I'll introduce you to the staff."

She followed him out into the main section of the store. By the cash register, an attractive young woman with shoulder-length blond hair was nosily chewing gum while talking with a man holding a broom. He was heavyset with brown curly hair and a hooked nose. His face was dotted with acne. The woman suddenly laughed at something the man said. They both straightened up and quieted as Mr. Handsome approached.

"Everyone, this is ... Tarantula. She's starting the night shift tonight."

Mr. Handsome stumbled over the pronunciation, again putting the emphasis on the second syllable. Tarantula hissed softly.

"Like the spider?" joked the man. The blond woman tittered.

How boundlessly clever these humans were. Tarantula arranged her face into the pleasant smile she had practiced in the mirror earlier that day. "It's Tar-an-TOO-la, with the stress on the third syllable. But you can just call me Tula." She hoped her voice sounded chipper.

"Taran … Tula recently moved here," continued Mr. Handsome. "She's going to be working the 11-7 graveyard shift. Please help her learn how to best assist our customers." He gestured towards the female. "This is Melanie, one of our cashiers."

The woman nodded her head slightly while making a popping sound with her gum.

"Paul takes care of stocking the shelves and keeping the store shipshape. He'll overlap with you most nights until 1 a.m."

"Welcome, Tula," Paul said with an easy grin. He was dressed in a dark green T-shirt that had a spiky animal printed in the center surrounded by the words, "Hedgehogs: Why Don't They Just Share The Hedge?"

"Melanie, Tula arrived early tonight, so if you have time, would you show her how to work the cash register?"

"Absolutely, Mr. Hanson," Melanie chirped, twisting her hair around her index finger.

"Paul, I'm sure you have work to do."

"Yes sir," Paul replied and immediately strolled away and began sweeping the nearest aisle.

Tarantula found an opening in the back of the stockade of gum and candy surrounding the register and stood next to Melanie.

"Like, you know, this is a really easy job," Melanie turned to her and said.

Tarantula tensed. She wasn't sure how to process this comment. Was Melanie saying she liked her job? How should Tarantula know already if the job was easy? She shrugged her shoulders, hoping that was an appropriate response.

"Okay, so, like, let me show you how to, you know, work the cash register."

Tarantula relaxed. She recalled hearing these repetitive speech mannerisms while watching videos of teenagers on the Internet. She should make the effort to incorporate these tics into her own communications to make her disguise more authentic.

"I would really, like, appreciate that," she replied.

She listened as Melanie went through the mechanics of working the cash register that Tarantula had already mastered by observing the cashier the night before. It was a good thing there wasn't much new to learn, because she found Melanie's constant hair flipping and gum cracking distracting.

After ten painful minutes it seemed as if Melanie was about to wrap things up, but she continued on to explain in detail the layout of the store. Tarantula had by then committed to memory the name, price, purpose, and placement of every item for sale. Taking advantage of one of Melanie's rare pauses, Tarantula quickly interjected, "Thanks so much, Melanie, this was, you know, really nice of you to help me learn about being a cashier. I'll bet you're eager to get going so I don't want to, like, keep you here any longer."

Melanie tossed her hair and squeaked, "Like, no problem! See you tomorrow. Good luck tonight!" She waved as she walked out of the store.

A short time after, Mr. Handsome exited as well. At the door he said, "If you have any problems, ask Paul. He knows how to work the cash register and he'll be here until 1. I'll see you at 7 a.m."

She nodded and gave him one of those smiles where her teeth showed. When the door closed, she settled onto the stool in front of the register. Paul walked over.

"You from around town?" he asked in a friendly way.

"I just moved here."

"From where?"

Beelzebub had warned her to keep things vague. "From further south," she said guardedly.

"Is that why you're wearing a turtleneck in August? It's insanely hot outside, how can you stand wearing that sweater?"

Tarantula was prepared for this. During her time on the Internet that afternoon she also researched medical conditions that would explain certain aspects of her appearance, in case the humans got nosy.

"I have trouble with my thyroid," she sighed. "It's a gland in my neck. I always feel cold." She cast her eyes to the side hoping to look uncomfortable.

"Oh," he said, embarrassed. "Sorry about that." After an awkward moment, he muttered, "Guess I should get back to sweeping the rest of the aisles."

Relieved that the questioning had stopped and she finally had a moment to herself, Tarantula turned to the register. Best to keep them all at arm's length. She'd already decided not to choose a co-worker as a victim. Too risky.

Only a few customers straggled in over the next two hours. It wasn't difficult to answer questions or ring up sales. At 1 a.m., Paul asked her if she needed any help, and when she said no, he left the store.

In the quiet, she strolled up and down the aisles. Ah, the mischief she could cause in a place like this. She wandered over to the housewares section where they stocked sewing notions and slid a packet of needles off of the bracket. There were so many possibilities. Perhaps mix some bleach into bottles of mouthwash? She drew out a needle and rehung the opened package behind the other packages of needles. Maybe swap the labels on the medications for constipation and diarrhea? She turned and walked down the next aisle to the area that housed contraceptives. She chose a box of condoms and began repeatedly poking the needle through the soft cardboard to the other side. No, she thought, she was not here for minor misdeeds. She put the box of condoms back on the shelf, walked to the register, and dropped the needle into the garbage can under the counter.

Later, a pale, thin, college-aged girl with black hair messily piled on top of her head burst into the store. Tarantula tracked her reflection in the large round mirror that hung from the ceiling, specifically placed to allow the staff to keep an eye on customers. The girl made a beeline to the food section, filled her arms with packages of cookies, brownies, and cupcakes, and ran to the register to dump everything she had gathered onto the counter in front of Tarantula. Then she headed down a different aisle, looked over her shoulder quickly, and slipped a bottle of laxative into her backpack. Returning to the register, she hesitated at a display of single-dose energy drink bottles and threw two of those onto her stack as well.

"How much?" she asked in a breathy voice.

Tarantula noticed that the girl's teeth were ragged and yellow. She rang up all of the items.

"Twenty-nine dollars and sixty-three cents."

The girl rummaged around in her backpack while Tarantula loaded the items into two bags. She saw the purple and white bottle of laxative swim under the girl's searching hand but said nothing. Finally, the girl fished out a rectangle of silver plastic and offered it to Tarantula. She avoided Tarantula's eyes when Tarantula handed back the card and asked her to sign the receipt.

"Thanks," the girl said and rushed out of the store.

Tarantula's gaze lingered on the exit. She doubted the girl was buying those treats to share with roommates at 2 a.m. Her teeth were in terrible shape, possibly due to frequent vomiting. She didn't think the laxative was for constipation either. A thief with an eating disorder. This human had potential.

At 4:40 a.m., the door swung open and a good-looking young man wearing a wrinkled gray Earl University T-shirt stumbled into the store. The reek of alcohol hit her nasal slits as he moved past the register. After a few moments he staggered up to the counter and slapped down a box of condoms. There were tiny holes in it.

Throw it away, a small voice nudged in her head. *Tell him to get another package.*

A bolt of electricity shot through her. No. Not this again. She forced down a surge of panic. How stupid she had been to think that her terrifying confrontation with Lucifer might have wiped out these sympathetic intrusions. She had not heard the voice for some time and had foolishly concluded the problem was gone.

"Hurry up, Sweetheart, I don't have all night," slurred the man. "Got a hot babe waiting for me. You know our motto, work hard, play hard." He swayed toward her and winked.

The Temptation Project was her chance to redeem her reputation. It had to succeed. This problem of hers must be controlled. She would prove to everyone, including herself, that she was a merciless, cold-hearted demon and a soldier of Lucifer.

"Enjoy your evening," she said with a smile as she put the condoms into a bag and handed it across the counter.

She would be on her guard from now on.

The Makeover

Beelzebub was sitting at the kitchen table when Tarantula arrived home that morning after her first shift. With a fork he pushed a yellow, curd-like substance around a greasy plate.

"That does not look appealing," she said.

He gazed up at her with forlorn eyes. "Do you think that observation has escaped me?" He jabbed at the gelatinous mound. "Taking in nourishment is one of many challenging aspects of possession. Usually, I enter the body of a high-ranking male, and servants prepare my meals for me. Your project has committed me to an isolated existence during which I must provide my own sustenance." He shook his head. "Why I agreed …," he muttered under his breath.

"You should get yourself a wife," she laughed. "Isn't that how it works up here?"

Beelzebub turned a light shade of green. "That is not funny, Tarantula. Yesterday afternoon, after I could no longer abide staying shut up in this house, I went for a walk around the neighborhood. No fewer than three middle-aged women attempted to engage me in conversation about nonsense. The word must be out that Bernard Smith has money and is unmarried. My strolls in the future will occur only under the cover of night."

She patted him on the shoulder. "Poor Uncle B. I can try to cook for you if you'd like."

"I sincerely doubt you will have any greater success at it than I have had. And a word of caution: if you do attempt to prepare something, do not use your flame. Stick with the oven or the stove."

She laughed again and sat down.

"You seem to be in annoyingly high spirits," he groaned.

"I had a good first night." She told him about the Earl University student and the box of condoms. That seemed to cheer him up somewhat. "And there is a prospect," she added.

A gleam came into Beelzebub's eyes. "Outstanding, Tarantula. That is fast work indeed. Have you any details to share?"

"Not yet, but I sense potential. I'll keep you posted."

She went upstairs to her room. These long gaps between working hours were going to be difficult to fill, especially as she felt uneasy out in broad daylight both because of the glare of the sun and the fragility of her disguise. She flopped down on the bed with a plan to spend the day researching topics on her phone and trying out some video games.

As twilight fell, she decided some attention to her personal hygiene was in order. After checking throughout the upstairs to ensure that all blinds were lowered and drapes were closed, she stripped off her boots, socks, pants, sweater, and turtleneck in her bedroom and eagerly ran into the bathroom. There, she gingerly removed her contact lenses. Rubbing and blinking her eyes, she reveled in seeing reflected in the mirror her orange irises and vertically slit pupils. And how marvelous it felt to free herself of the itchy wig. She placed the wig over its inflatable stand on the shelf above the toilet, then gave her head a good scratching. With a fistful of tissues, she wiped the greasy makeup from her face, neck, and hands. But by far, the best part of the unmasking process was peeling off the miserable body suit. She lowered the zipper, snaked out one arm then the other, and eased the fabric over her shoulders and down to her waist. Out sprang her cramped wings, which she stretched luxuriously to their full extent. Now this was something to look forward to every day. She tugged the body suit the rest of the way down and stripped it off of her legs. Turning her back to the mirror, she admired her sleek tail as she whipped it to and fro a few times. Kicking the body suit into a corner, she stepped into the shower and turned it on full blast at its hottest setting. Beelzebub was right: it was a deficient stand-in for an acid bath, but it would have to do.

Later, she laboriously reversed the process as she readied herself for work. Sifting through the clothes in her closet, she pulled out a patterned jacket that went well with her blue jeans. She plucked one of her many black turtlenecks from the dresser drawer. She didn't care if people thought wearing turtlenecks in July was strange; they kept her from freezing in the air-conditioned store. She wriggled, writhed, and packed herself back into the hateful body suit. Then it was clothes on, wig snapped securely into place, contacts in, makeup slathered, boots tied, and she was ready to go.

"Don't go breaking any hearts," she yelled to Beelzebub as she closed the front door behind her and went out into the night.

Across the street, the tall girl with the dog was loitering around on her lawn. Great goblins, what was with her? Tarantula walked briskly down the sidewalk, noting that the girl and dog had crossed the street and were now trailing behind her.

She didn't like this one bit. After another block she looked back and saw the girl was gaining on her. She abruptly turned to the right and cut through a yard to a parallel street. When she checked again, she was relieved to see that the girl and dog had not followed her. Rattled, she tracked back to her usual route and entered the pharmacy.

She was about fifteen minutes early. Paul and Melanie were talking by the cash register as she walked by.

"Hey, Tula," Paul said.

She nodded in their direction and went over to the magazine rack. With her hyperacute senses, it wasn't difficult for her to overhear their conversation.

"Like, what's with the turtleneck?" Melanie sniggered. "Who does she think she is, like Steve Jobs or something?"

"Shhh, she'll hear you," Paul answered quietly. "She told me she has some kind of gland problem in her neck. She's always cold."

"Oh," said Melanie. She thoughtfully snapped her gum a few times. Then she asked Paul if he would cover the register and walked over to the magazine rack.

"Hey, Tula, how did it, you know, go last night?"

Tarantula looked up from the issue of *Popular Mechanics* she was digesting.

"Oh," she shrugged, "it was, you know, okay."

"Hey, like, if you've got a sec, come back with me to the employee bathroom, I want to ask you something."

Melanie had a large purse hanging off of her shoulder. Not knowing quite what to do, Tarantula obediently followed her through the Employees Only door. Melanie walked down the hallway and pushed open a door on the right that had a silhouette of a person wearing a dress on it. This must be the bathroom for females. That was something she hadn't thought about. If Mr. Handsome ever asked her to work a daytime shift when other employees were around, she would have to remember to visit this room from time to time, to fake excretory functions.

Inside there were two sinks and three stalls. Melanie propped the bag next to one of the sinks and faced her. "Tula, like, Paul shared with me that you have, you know, gland problems," she said.

Tarantula was caught completely by surprise. Did these humans have no respect for privacy?

"Um ... yeah," was all she could blurt out.

"Well, like, I want to, you know, help!" Melanie squeaked. "Does your gland problem affect your looks?

Because, like, I couldn't help noticing how thick your foundation is. And is that, like, a wig you're wearing?"

Tarantula's eye slits widened in alarm. She had worked so hard to look like a human, and here this idiot of a girl was seeing through her disguise in, what, twenty-four hours? This was not good.

"M-my hypothyroidism," she stuttered, "makes my skin really dry and scaly and also my hair falls out, so, like, I'm trying to look the best I can."

"Well," gushed Melanie, "I'm planning on going to beauty school and I would, you know, love to give you, like, a makeover."

Tarantula stared at Melanie. It took her a moment to realize that this human wasn't suspicious of her camouflage after all. She was just trying to be nice. What did Melanie have to gain by offering to help her improve her looks? This was puzzling. Although it was risky, Tarantula decided it would be foolish to refuse Melanie's assistance and potentially alienate her.

"Sure," she said with fake exuberance while forcing her cheeks up as high as they would go.

"Yes!" squealed the girl as she clapped her hands and made small jumping movements. But as Melanie scanned Tarantula's face more closely, her smile faded. "Um, we're, like, going to need more time than, you know, I thought. How about we meet here tomorrow night at like 10:30 and I'll bring my full makeup kit. Paul can, you know, cover the register for a half hour. I'm going to make you look awesome!" She snapped her gum for emphasis.

Tarantula's face was still locked in a smile.

"Like, fantastic!" she croaked.

The next night, when Tarantula entered the pharmacy at 10:30, Melanie excitedly waved to her from behind the cash register.

"Hi, Tula," she warbled, "like, see you in a min."

Tarantula waved back. It was difficult to contain the snort that was on the cusp of erupting from her nasal slits. What a colossal waste of time this human fuss was about makeup. It was bad enough she had to deal with applying the concealer to her hands and face every day. In addition, the question of why Melanie was so keen to help had bedeviled her for the past twenty-four hours.

Tarantula shook her head and sighed. Oh well, how bad could thirty minutes with Melanie be? It was worth a small amount of aggravation to establish some rapport with the girl. Tarantula continued onward to the employee bathroom. A few minutes later, the door swung open, and Melanie walked in.

"Okay, like, let's do this!" Melanie said breathlessly. After propping her bag open on the countertop between the sinks, she began unpacking bottles, tubes, pots, swabs, brushes, and other paraphernalia. Tarantula was horrified.

"First, you have to wash all of that foundation off of your face," Melanie ordered.

What? The girl was already pushing her too far.

"I can't do that," Tarantula snapped.

Melanie stopped arranging the clutter and looked up. "Like, why not?"

Tarantula could see that agreeing to this makeover had been a mistake. The interaction was too close for comfort. But as she was now trapped in the bathroom with Melanie, she had to keep her cool.

"Because I'm very self-conscious about the way my skin looks," Tarantula said in a softer tone. "Can't you just point to things and then I'll know, like, what to buy?" She raised her eyebrows, tilted her head, and twisted the neckline of her turtleneck hoping to look pitiful.

Melanie shrugged her shoulders in frustration but seemed to accept the explanation. She launched into a five-minute lecture on how to apply foundation and waved around a bottle of tan liquid that she promised was miraculous. After a great deal of begging, Tarantula allowed her to apply some eyeliner to the top of her eye slits with a wand. She was careful not to let Melanie touch her face with her hand. After a lot of dabbing, Melanie stepped back and stared at Tarantula.

"Wow," she exhaled, "I am, like, really talented."

She was so ecstatic about her skills that Tarantula reluctantly let her brush on some blush while carefully maintaining a space between them.

"Like, voila!" Melanie said, stepping to the side to allow Tarantula to fully view herself in the mirror.

She had to admit, the girl had made some significant improvements.

"Tula, you look fabulous!" Melanie declared. "Here, like, you can keep these products, I bought them for you."

Tarantula stiffened. Melanie had gone to the trouble of buying cosmetics specifically for her. This was deeply unsettling.

So nice of her, murmured the voice.

Get out of my head! Go away! She forced her eyes to focus on Melanie's face. Probably right now she was supposed to be saying something.

"Th ... thank you," she managed to choke out. "That is so ... kind of you, Melanie." The words were like bitter ash on her tongue.

"Like, no prob, I had fun! I know, next time we'll go to the mall and get your ears pierced," Melanie said as she skipped out into the hallway.

Tarantula stood speechless as the bathroom door swung shut.

The Hook

Two nights later, the pale skinny girl was back. Around 2 a.m. she hurried in and circled around to the back of the store. Tarantula pretended to count dollar bills in the register drawer while tracking her movements in the ceiling mirror. The girl seemed agitated. She paced once more across the back wall and then trotted towards the register.

"Do you have a bathroom here I can use?" she inquired anxiously.

"It's for employees only," Tarantula replied.

The girl muttered a swear word under her breath. "It's kind of an emergency," she pressed, "could you please let me use it?"

Tarantula paused. There was no one else in the store. And it was time to move forward with the Temptation Project. "Okay, follow me."

The girl hovered closely behind Tarantula as she led her through the Employees Only door and along the corridor to the bathroom on the right. She gestured towards the door and the girl scurried in. Standing in the hallway, Tarantula could hear through the thin wall the predictable sounds of vomiting. Then a toilet flushed, water ran in the sink, paper towels were pulled from the dispenser, and the girl emerged.

"Thanks," she muttered, staring at the floor.

"There are better ways to lose weight, you know," Tarantula said.

The girl glanced up. "I don't know what you're talking about," she croaked. "I have a virus."

"Is that the reason you walked all the way to a store to throw up in the middle of the night?"

The girl was silent.

"Listen, I know how you feel," Tarantula purred. "But you're never going to get what you want by binging and purging. I can show you how to get rid of your fat a much better way."

The girl's bloodshot eyes filled with tears. Bingo.

"I'm just so tired," the girl whispered miserably, sinking down the wall into a sitting position on the floor. "I'm tired of trying to get money to pay for all the food I buy, tired of stuffing my face, tired of trying to find places to puke where people won't hear me. It's not even working, I'm still a disgusting cow."

If anything, she was on the too-thin side. Clearly her perception of her body was badly distorted. Splendid.

"I understand how ugly you feel and how hard it is to reach the weight you want," Tarantula said soothingly. "Let me help you."

"Really? But you're so slim and, I don't know, you seem so confident. Have you ever been through this?"

Tarantula was taken aback. She'd received a compliment from a human. Unexpected pleasure washed over her. Irked, she brushed the thought aside and focused on laying her groundwork.

"What you really crave isn't food, its control over your body and your hunger," she said in a tranquilizing murmur. "To me, all food is gross. I've trained myself not to eat, and I feel great and never have to worry about my weight. If you want to talk about how I do it, I'd be glad to hang out."

"You would? That would be incredible," the girl gasped, getting up from the floor, wiping her eyes, and even smiling a little. "Everyone at Earl University always seems to be so happy and perfect. It's hard being in summer session here and trying to fit in. I haven't made any friends."

"Where are you from?" Tarantula asked gently.

"Idaho."

"Does your family know you are struggling?"

"No, I can't really talk to them about this."

Tarantula ticked things off in her mind. Young college student: check. Far away from home: check. Isolated, no friends: check. Parental involvement minimal: check. Self-loathing: check. This was almost too good to be true.

"Tell you what," she said. "I get off at 7 a.m. After I hit the sack for a while, why don't we meet somewhere on campus and talk more? Maybe this afternoon?"

"That would be amazing," the girl said eagerly.

"Okay. I'll meet you outside the gym, say, at 1:00?" Tarantula didn't think it would be difficult to locate the athletic complex. "My name is Tula, by the way."

"Mine's Maria. You're a lifesaver, Tula, thanks so much for letting me use the bathroom, I really needed to get rid of what I ate earlier tonight."

"No problem. Don't eat again until we talk, okay?"

The girl nodded and smiled weakly. Together they walked back towards the front of the store.

"See you at 1:00," Tarantula said, stepping behind the register.

The girl looked over her shoulder, raised a hand, and left.

As she climbed the steps to her house a few hours later, Tarantula glanced over at the home across the street. Did the blinds in one of the upstairs windows just move? She hurriedly unlocked the door and went inside. Beelzebub was slouched on the sofa in the living room staring at the television with a dazed look. On the screen, a group of young women wearing low-cut gowns were clustered around a man holding a bunch of long-stemmed roses.

"Hey," she said, while closing and locking the door. "Something interesting?"

Beelzebub slowly swung his head around. He looked terrible. His eyes were sunken and glassy. A pale sheen of sweat covered his flabby face. He was wearing the same clothes he had put on the day of their arrival. Chances were good he hadn't yet washed the body he was inhabiting. Bits of her makeup were still embedded in the whiskers on his right cheek.

"I sincerely question whether I will be able to endure three more weeks of this," he rasped. "I have read every publication in this structure. Not an impressive selection, I can assure you. The newspaper is filled with reminders of the innumerable opportunities for promoting evil in the world that I am currently neglecting. The television programs are brain damaging; I do not understand how humans can bear to watch them. If I leave the house, I am stalked by females who seem to have an infinite capacity for tracking my scent."

"Speaking of your scent, when was the last time you took a shower and changed your clothes?" she asked, walking into the living room.

Beelzebub frowned darkly at her. "This is not a role I am relishing, Tarantula. Please tell me you have made some progress on the Temptation Project."

"As a matter of fact, I have," she said, dropping into one of the armchairs and switching off the television with the remote just as the man on the screen was ogling one of the women and drawing her into a bedroom. "I'm meeting with my first prospect this afternoon."

Beelzebub sat up straighter on the couch. "Do tell, I could use a boost."

"She is an unhappy, isolated, and insecure Earl University summer student."

"Very nice. And your plan?"

"She has an eating disorder."

Beelzebub's face fell. "Hardly a reason for being brought before Lucifer, wouldn't you agree?" he scoffed.

Tarantula was silent. She had expected Beelzebub to be more enthusiastic about her potential victim.

"Tarantula," he said more gently, "you have taken on a project that you will begin to realize may be more complex than you had initially envisioned. With the mortals you engage in the Temptation Project, you face two major tasks. The first is to befriend your targets in order to gain their trust, so that you can successfully tempt them to commit acts of wrongdoing. These acts must be sufficiently evil so as to damn them for all eternity to Hell. Religions on The Surface are numerous and interpretations of sin are varied. The safest approach is to aim for transgressions that are common to most beliefs, such as killing, cheating, lying, stealing, that sort of thing."

"I saw her steal something in the store," Tarantula said hopefully.

"A positive start," Beelzebub encouraged. "You can continue to build upon that weakness. But tempting a human to commit a grave offense is not enough to satisfy the goal of your project. You promoted this enterprise to Lucifer by promising to deliver more adolescent souls to Hell. Therefore, your second task will be to ensure that your victims die soon after sinning. It would be poor form to allow them time to redeem themselves."

How shallow her thinking had been. Beelzebub's mapping out of her responsibilities made her realize that she hadn't considered in any detail how she would actually carry out her pledge to Lucifer. Significant sinning and rapid dying. That would be her new mantra.

"Now," he continued, "as you are aware, most human adolescents are frustratingly healthy. Their most frequent causes of death are murder, suicide, and accidents. You can use this knowledge to consider exit strategies for each of your targets. However, under no circumstances are you to physically manipulate the lifespan of a mortal. You may tempt, but you must never inflict death."

No inflicting death. Tarantula contemplated Beelzebub's words. This information would assist her in her planning. Almost a week had gone by. It was time to shift into higher gear.

"The girl is a thief," she said slowly as she rose from the chair and began pacing back and forth across the room. "As I get to know her better, I may find other desirable behaviors to encourage." She looked up to see Beelzebub nodding at her. "I'm also certain she has an eating disorder. If I can convince her to severely restrict her intake, she could end up with a fatal medical complication."

"Now you are on the right track," Beelzebub said. He studied the floor as he rubbed his unshaven face with his hand. "I can see," he sighed, "how my one-month time limitation on the Temptation Project may impose significant pressure upon you."

She stopped pacing and faced him. "Yes, it definitely does. I would like to reopen the conversation we had regarding your terms. Can't you give me at least two months on The Surface?"

"Impossible," he said, waving her suggestion away. "I feel as if I am trapped in one of your notorious torture narratives."

"Then I beg you to reduce the projected number of victims. It is unreasonable for you to expect me to accomplish the tasks you've outlined for six marks in the twenty-four days I have remaining."

Beelzebub stroked his chin. "What would you consider feasible?"

"Two victims. I think I could manage that."

Beelzebub exhaled a long breath. "Lucifer will be less impressed with your bringing just two souls to him, Tarantula. If you want him to believe the Temptation Project is a valid conceit, you must show him significant results."

"Two souls to him in four weeks," she pushed. "Certainly, that will prove the project has potential. Two souls will allow me to concentrate my efforts."

"As you wish," Beelzebub grudgingly acquiesced. "But please make your successes as grisly as possible. There is an entertainment factor here to consider." He heaved himself off of the couch. "And speaking of grisly, I suppose I should shower and shave."

"And brush your teeth," she called to his retreating back.

Tarantula was relieved she had been able to convince Beelzebub to reduce the number of victims to two. But time was ticking away. She ran up the stairs to her bedroom, eager to read everything she could find on the Internet about anorexia nervosa.

Prospect Number Two

Tarantula left the house at 11:30 a.m. to give herself plenty of time to get oriented to the Earl University campus and to locate the gym. Fortunately, it was a cloudy day. With her sunglasses on and an Earl University baseball cap fitted over her wig, the glare of daylight was tolerable. She carried an umbrella with her as well. It wouldn't look good to be caught in a storm and have her makeup running in rivulets off of her hands and face.

As she walked down the street, she sensed a presence behind her. Glancing over her shoulder, she saw the tall girl from across the street approximately a half block behind her. The dog was not with her. Devil's damnation, this human was becoming a nuisance. She quickened her pace and glanced around for alternative routes. Just as she was about to steal another peek, a voice right behind her made her jump.

"I know what you are," the girl called out.

Tarantula whirled around. "What?" was all she could choke out.

"I know what you are," the girl repeated, staring directly into her sunglasses.

Tarantula's mind began to race. Had she forgotten a part of her costume? She mentally ticked off the components: wig, contacts, makeup, bodysuit, clothes, shoes; they were all in place. Was her tail loose? She casually ran her hand over the back of her pants and felt the flattened coil safely secured. How could this be happening?

"I … I don't know what you're talking about," she snapped, trying to buy some time.

She looked more carefully at the girl. Something was different about her. Her voice was lower than the other female voices she had heard. A thick layer of concealer had been applied to her face and neck. Was there a hint of a beard showing through the makeup?

"You don't have to hide from me," the young woman said in a more friendly tone, reaching to touch Tarantula's shoulder. "I've been watching you, and I think we both may be going through the same thing. Perhaps we can be friends."

Tarantula sidestepped the outstretched hand and forced a smile. What was happening here? Was this another demon in disguise? Had Lucifer sent other workers to The Surface to assist with the Temptation Project? Her thoughts spun. How should she handle this?

"Transitioning can be really hard, especially down in these parts," the girl drawled on with a strong Southern accent. "I've noticed your wig, the makeup, your bulky clothes, and, well ...."

The girl's face suddenly fell and she raised an extra-large hand to cover her opened mouth. "Oh my god, I'm wrong! I'm wrong!" she exclaimed dramatically. "I can see by the look on your face. Have I offended you? I am so, so sorry!"

The girl again reached out to touch Tarantula, but she pivoted in time to avoid the second attempt at physical contact. Meanwhile, she latched onto the word "transitioning," quickly sifting through her knowledge base of adolescent development. Of course. She put together the tall body frame, large hands, low voice, and thick makeup. Chances were good this person had been assigned a male gender growing up and was now converting to a female. Relief sharpened into keen interest. She had read that adolescents changing their gender identity were often challenged by isolation, harassment, and discrimination. She eyed the young human before her who was now pleading for forgiveness. This mortal was looking for an ally. She quickly rearranged her features and gave the girl a shy smile.

"You haven't offended me," she said lightly. "You're right, we probably do have a lot of things in common. But I think the reason I'm wearing heavy makeup may be different than yours."

The tall female stopped apologizing long enough to say, "You're not angry?"

"Not at all," Tarantula reassured her. "I'd like to talk more, but I have to go meet a friend at Earl University right now. Will you be around this afternoon, say, around 4:00?"

"Oh honey, you better believe it," breathed the girl. "Should I come over to your house, or would you rather come to mine?"

"I'll come to your house," Tarantula cut in swiftly. "My name is Tula, what's yours?"

"Skyler, Skyler Diggs," the woman gushed. "I have really wanted to meet you, Tula, ever since you moved in. I am so happy I got up the nerve today to talk to you."

"Me too," replied Tarantula. "You'll never know how thrilled I am. But I have to go now. See you then!"

She headed back down the sidewalk. This was shaping up to be a busy day.

She arrived on the Earl University campus with plenty of time to spare. This was her first opportunity to observe students outside of the confines of the pharmacy. Walking along paths that led past ivy-covered brick buildings with massive white columns, she noted the relaxed attitudes of the students lying on blankets, throwing plastic discs, or kissing under trees. Music blared from dormitory windows and the air was thick with the smell of marijuana. As she considered the freedom these young humans had regarding sex, alcohol, and drugs, she appreciated what gold mines of temptation colleges truly were. If Lucifer could be convinced that the Temptation Project was legit, she would make sure she placed a demon in every college and university on The Surface. The Adolescent Torture Area would be brimming with souls in no time. But she was getting ahead of herself; there was work to do.

Using the map function on her phone, Tarantula made her way to the gym without difficulty and sat outside on a bench. Students streamed in and out of the swinging doors. Although their bodies showed much variation, their dress did not. The males wore shorts and T-shirts, often with Earl University imprints on them.

The women wore tight-fitting pants and tops that looked similar to her body suit. She doubted they were as uncomfortable as she was, though.

A child holding the hand of an adult toddled out of the building wearing a shirt that featured a crude drawing of a devil on its front. That caught her attention. She focused more carefully on the writing on the clothing of the people parading in and out. Apparently, the Earl University mascot was a green devil. She snorted, wondering if Beelzebub's selection of a home base near this university was one of his lame jokes.

Maria ran up to her at 1:10, breathless and disheveled. "So sorry I'm late," she gasped, "class ran over. Let's go somewhere we can talk." She led Tarantula to a corner of campus that merged into wooded running trails.

Tarantula had been worried that she would have to dig deeply into her bag of tricks to get Maria to talk about herself. It turned out that concern was unfounded. As soon as the quiet of the woods surrounded them, Maria spontaneously began to spill her story.

"I've had a problem with eating since 7th grade."

She paused. Tarantula remained quiet.

"Growing up, I never thought much about my weight or my body. I ate whatever I wanted. My parents, you know, made sure I had a decent breakfast, lunch, and dinner every day, but I had candy, dessert, soda, that kind of junk all the time. Then in the summer before 7th grade, everything started to change."

There was another silence. Tarantula was good at being patient.

"I guess I was going through puberty and stuff. I didn't change anything about the way I was eating, but I started to gain weight. I could tell it was really bugging my parents, because all of a sudden we quit having dessert after dinner, and they kept bringing up how important it was to eat healthy. It was way annoying."

Two squirrels noisily chased each other around a tree trunk next to the path and scurried into the undergrowth.

"Around the same time, my best friend said she was going to try out for the cross country team. She told me she was doing it because boys liked girls with toned bodies. I didn't know what that meant, but when school started, I went out for the team with her. I was kind of surprised that I made it. Turned out, the coach was a great guy. He helped me with my running form, created special workouts for me, and suggested I up my energy intake by drinking protein shakes."

Maria bent down, picked up a leaf, and ripped it into small pieces as she walked.

"The protein shakes tasted delicious, and they were filling. Sometimes I wouldn't eat any dinner because after I had a shake in the afternoon, I wasn't hungry. Well, with all the exercise and skipped meals, my weight started to go down. My clothes weren't so tight anymore and I liked the way I looked. You know, kind of thin but with muscles. But the best part was that my running times were improving. The more weight I dropped, the faster I ran."

She looked sideways at Tarantula, who gave her an encouraging nod.

"My parents started to get worried about me, but I was feeling great. When the cross country season was over, my coach invited me to run with the indoor track team. I went out and bought some new clothes because my old ones were getting too baggy, and my friends told me I looked like a model in them. Boys who never paid any attention to me before were hanging around my locker in between classes. Kids I barely knew cheered me on at track meets. It was amazing. I figured I had a good thing going, so I stopped eating solid food completely and only had the protein shakes every day. I became obsessed with getting my weight down as low as possible. One day, I was working out on the track, and I got this really bad pain in my foot. I could barely walk.

My mother took me to the doctor, and that's when things began to fall apart."

Maria took a deep breath, then continued.

"The doctor did an x-ray and said I had a stress fracture from all the running. But he also noticed that my bones looked kind of see-through on the film. So he started asking me all sorts of questions about eating and my period (it had stopped months ago, which was awesome), and made me get on the scale twice. Then he talked to my mom in private in his office. When they came back into the exam room they said I couldn't run track any more until I got my weight up. I couldn't believe it. I was so mad."

She veered off the path to a flat slab of rock in the underbrush and sat down. Tarantula hoisted herself up next to her.

"Well, I'll spare you the details of the fights I had with my parents, doctors, and coaches throughout the rest of junior high and high school. My parents said they wouldn't let me go away to college unless I was at a healthy weight. Finally, I agreed to enroll in an eating disorder program. I forced myself to gain weight, thinking it was the only way to escape from all of the adults constantly watching me. Once I got to college last fall, it was a relief to have a fresh start, you know? But things there were harder than I thought they would be. I felt a lot of pressure to make friends and have a boyfriend, and my courses were tough. The dining halls had stuff like all-you-can-eat ice cream, and at night someone on my floor was always ordering pizza. Then there were the frat parties on weekends. Everyone was doing shots and drinking beer; there was no way I could just stand around and not drink. I gained even more weight. That's when I started making myself throw up. It would make me feel better for a while, but then I would get super hungry and stuff my face with tons of junk food."

Maria's shoulders slumped as she stared down at the ground. A few tears plopped onto the leaves at the base of the rock. Remembering Skyler's thwarted gestures that morning, Tarantula tentatively reached over and lightly patted Maria's shoulder. It felt weird to touch a human.

"Then things got crazier and crazier." Maria was having difficulty choking out the words now. "When the dining hall was closed, I started scrounging for food wherever I could get it. I figured out how to rig the vending machines in the library to get free candy. Sometimes I stole from the Campus Store. Then when I ate all the cookies my roommate's mother had sent her for her birthday, she went ballistic. She said she knew I was taking her money to buy food. I felt so disgusting and ashamed. So, I got a job on campus, paid her back, and got better at hiding what I was doing. I had to drop two of my courses that semester because I was so stressed. That's why I'm here taking a summer course at Earl University."

It appeared Maria had finished speaking for now. The information had been tedious but useful. Tarantula rummaged around in her brain for a phrase of compassion.

"That must have been really hard for you," she tried.

It seemed to do the trick. Maria lifted her head and looked at Tarantula. "It feels so good to talk to you, Tula," she said, wiping her eyes. "I've been keeping all of this inside of me. My parents have no idea what's going on. As long as nobody contacts them from the university, they're happy."

"Your parents don't understand what you need," murmured Tarantula. "Your doctors don't either."

"That's what I've been thinking," Maria said, her voice rising. "It's like you can read my mind."

"You should follow your own instincts."

It was in this fashion that Tarantula began to spin her web. First, she placed her bridge and anchor threads.

"Remember how good it felt when you were thin? Think about the power you had when you controlled exactly what you ate. The pounds melted away, right?

You were beautiful, admired by everyone. You can have all that back again."

"I can?" Maria said.

"Of course, you can," Tarantula confidently answered, as she went about setting up her frame threads. "You did it back then and you can do it now. You don't have to worry about your bones because you're no longer running track. You can decide what you will eat, and more importantly, what you're not going to eat."

"But I've gotten so used to binging any time day or night. How can I just stop?"

As Tarantula spoke to Maria in a hypnotic drone, she continued to steadily weave her trap. The first radial thread she placed was the suggestion of a strict exercise routine. The next thread was the highly restrictive dietary plan. The third was the extraction of a promise from Maria that she would have no interaction with any medical personnel. There were threads for lying to her parents, classmates, and professors about her eating. Finally, she created the sticky central capture spiral by impressing upon Maria that only she, Tarantula, could help her reclaim those halcyon days when she was thin and in control.

By the time they got back to the gym, Maria seemed calm and determined. They agreed to get together every day in the late morning after Maria's class.

"I can't thank you enough, Tula," she said as she typed Tarantula's contact information into her phone. "You've saved me."

Tarantula's lips curled into a rare genuine smile. She loved irony.

"Remember, you can call me any time, day or night, I'm literally always awake."

It was one of the few things she had said all afternoon that hadn't been a lie.

Tightening The Webs

An eye peered through the sliver of space between the front door and its frame almost immediately after Tarantula knocked later that afternoon.

"Oh, I was worried you wouldn't come, but you're here!" Skyler said excitedly as she opened the door wider and waved Tarantula inside.

She turned, shut the door, and slid the bolt lock back into place. While Skyler was busy with the door, Tarantula did a quick inspection. She was tall, probably six feet or so. Her shoulder-length brown hair had an unnatural, stiff appearance, as if it had been ironed. Her baggy white T-shirt was bunched up over pink sweatpants. The slippers on her large feet looked as if she had murdered two rabbits and flattened their bodies with the same iron she had used on her hair.

"Why were you peeking out of your door?" Tarantula asked. "Are you worried about something?"

"Hon, you don't know the half of it," Skyler said, flapping her hand up and down once. "I'll tell you all about it. Come on upstairs."

A small black and white dog ran in from another room and approached Tarantula. It sniffed at her tentatively. A low growl began deep in its throat.

"That's Buddy," Skyler said with obvious affection.

Tarantula couldn't fathom the human need for pets. Nasty, dirty, annoying things. When Skyler turned around, she kicked at the dog and it scurried away.

As she followed Skyler across the entryway and up the stairs, she glanced around. This house didn't look much different from the one she was occupying with Beelzebub. She could see the living room with its requisite couch plus TV, and got a glimpse of the dining room that had the expected rectangular table surrounded by ugly upholstered chairs. On the way up the stairs there were numerous framed photographs of smiling people arranged on the walls. Those were definitely missing from her place.

Once they reached the upstairs landing, Skyler gestured towards one of the open doors and said, "This is my room."

Tarantula followed her inside.

"My parents are still at work and my sister stays late after school for cheerleading practice, so we have the house all to ourselves," she said as she flung herself onto her bed. She landed on a pink flowered sheet heaped in the center of a large mattress. Two flowered pillows were propped against a pink wicker headboard, and a fluffy pink blanket was lying half on the bed and half on the pink carpet. The curtains, wallpaper, and most of the stuffed animals that covered every inch of available surface were all some shade of pink.

"Nice room," Tarantula said, turning her back to Skyler and pretending to look more closely at the bookshelves so that her eye-rolling would go unseen. She strolled around, searching for a place to sit that wasn't the bed. In the corner of the room was a green and pink inflatable armchair that looked like the kind of thing one would find in a swimming pool. She dragged it into the middle of the room and cautiously lowered herself onto the seat.

"So, what's your story?" Skyler asked abruptly, sitting up, cross-legged.

Tarantula was still rocking around trying to find the center of gravity in the pool float when she heard Skyler's question. This human certainly had a direct style of communication. But Tarantula wasn't interested in Skyler learning much about her. Her purpose here today was to mine Skyler's angst. That shouldn't be a problem, she reasoned, because humans apparently loved to talk about themselves in excruciating detail.

"Um, you first," she encouraged.

Just a dab of curiosity was all it took.

"Okay, here goes," Skyler said, grabbing one of the flowered pillows and hugging it to her chest. "You see, I always knew I was somehow very special."

Tarantula did her best to make her peace with the chair. With an opening statement like that, she could tell getting through this conversation was going to require an enormous amount of staying power.

"For as long as I can remember, I was the one taking care of other people. Even as a child, I was watching out for my mother, father, and baby sister. It was as if I had my own personal radar for their problems. I knew when they were sad, or lonely, or frustrated, and I felt it was my job to make things better for them."

Skyler paused, perhaps hoping for some sort of response. But Tarantula had learned during her earlier chat with Maria that employing a technique of quiet expectation was a highly effective strategy for drawing people out. She leaned forward in her chair towards Skyler to signal her rapt attention. Her change in equilibrium reignited the battle with the pool float.

Skyler fell backwards on the bed and continued talking while staring at the ceiling. "I didn't feel that way only about my family. I had it with friends, teachers, classmates, with everyone. I was sensitive about a lot of stuff. I could tell that there was something in me that made me different, but I couldn't figure out what it was."

Skyler sat up and began picking at the plush blanket. "You've probably already figured out that when I was little, no one planned for me to grow up to be the glamorous female you see before you today." She gestured with her hand in a curving motion from the top of her head to the bottom of her torso and smiled ruefully. "It took me years and a lot of work to get where I am now. I was raised as a boy. But right from the start, I didn't want to play with boy things like trucks and guns. All I wanted were dolls. It bothered my parents when I asked for them for my birthdays, and they continued to buy me baseball bats and junk like that instead. So, I used my sister's dolls in secret. My father signed me up for Boy Scouts and Pop Warner football, hoping I'd toughen up, but I hated it. I'm sure I was a constant embarrassment to him."

Skyler rolled over on her belly and stuffed the pillow under her chin. "As I grew older, things got worse. At school I was teased by the other kids, especially the boys, because I wasn't interested in sports and just wanted to be with the girls. But they didn't want me hanging around them either. Basically, I had no friends. When I was in 6th grade, it got so bad that my parents took me to see a psychologist. At first I didn't tell her anything, but when she asked me during one session if I had ever tried on my sister's clothing, it was like a door opening. Nobody knew about that. Somehow this lady could see the real me. That was a turning point."

This called for an exclamation. "Wow," Tarantula remarked.

"After months of hard work together, she helped me realize that inside of me was a female trying to get out. And when I allowed myself to think in those terms, everything else began to make sense. When my psychologist and I finally told my parents that I was trans, they took it hard. But she gave them information to read and helped us find support groups. Now they understand, although I can tell they're nervous about what it will mean in the long run, like dealing with hormones and surgery. My sister has been totally cool and in my corner right from the start."

Bloody boogers, hissed Tarantula to herself. This was not the tale she was hoping to hear. It was sickening, with all its support this and understanding that. Maybe some dirt would surface soon. She made her head bob up and down while she forced herself to wait.

"In the summer before my junior year of high school, I felt ready to come out. My psychologist, parents, and I decided together that transferring to a new high school might make my transition smoother. I let my hair grow, completely redid my wardrobe, and began referring to myself with feminine pronouns. It was terrifying, but so freeing. My therapist was amazing. She helped me to see that the people who were nasty to me were ignorant; they just didn't know any better. It hasn't been easy, but I am so much happier now."

Skyler stopped talking and was playing with the fringe on her blanket. It was necessary for Tarantula to utter something substantial.

"Incredible," she said, struggling to hide her exasperation, "thanks for sharing all of this with me, Skyler, it is quite a story."

And a huge waste of her time, she fumed. A caretaking-type adolescent with a supportive family did not sound like the sort of human she was seeking to become her second target. Time to cut her losses and leave. There was just one small thing nagging in the back of her mind.

"I'm happy things are going better for you now" she lied. "But if everything is so great, what was with the nerves at the front door?"

Skyler got up off her bed and walked slowly across the room to the set of shelves against the wall. She picked up a pink and white spotted giraffe, held it up to her face, and began speaking to it.

"We hate him, we hate him to pieces, don't we?" she demanded of the stuffed toy.

"What? Who?" Tarantula asked.

Skyler placed the giraffe back on the shelf, turned around, and sat down on the carpet. "There's this guy I've known since I was a kid. He used to torment me in school. He'd get all the boys on the playground to call me names like 'girl,' 'fag,' and 'queer bait.' I'm pretty sure he and his buddies egged my house once."

Her voice dropped to a whisper. "In junior high, I found a doll in my locker with a noose around its neck and a note pinned to it that said 'pervert' on it. I'm positive it was him. He was one of the reasons I switched schools." She began chewing on an already abused fingernail. "There was also a rumor that he killed a kitten, just to show off to his friends."

Now this was more like it. Tarantula, trying to tamp down her surging optimism, realized that she should react negatively to the kitten thing.

"That is awful," she said, raising her eyebrows and opening her mouth.

"Yeah, well it gets worse." Skyler hesitated, her voice going even lower. "After I graduated from high school this past spring, I decided to enroll in Deadham Community College to study theater. I signed up for a summer course to get a jump on my requirements. On my first day on campus who do I run into but this creep. He immediately recognized me, saw that I was now out as a woman, and let out this big whoop. Then he told me I was a freak, and that I'd better not show my face on campus again. But Tula, the school has a terrific theater program and my parents have already paid my tuition. I can't just not go. I try to avoid him, but it's a small place. He is so cruel to me, you would not believe it."

Water began to trickle down Skyler's cheeks. It appeared this would be a day of tears.

"When he sees me, he follows me around campus saying slurs and threats under his breath," Skyler sniffed. "I want to try out for a role in the winter theater production, but I'm afraid to because I worry he might sabotage the show." She wiped her eyes and dropped her hands into her lap. "But the worst part is, I think he showed a knife to me last week."

Tula didn't have to fake her expression of surprise this time. A knife! How delicious.

"What?" she gasped.

"I was on campus two weeks ago because a classmate invited me to a party. I was having such an enjoyable time until I heard someone say right by my ear, 'Hey pretty lady, want to dance?' I turned around and it was him, staring at me. Tula, it was so creepy. I tried to get away, but the room was really crowded. He flashed some sort of metal object in his hand and said I needed to have something cut off. I pushed my way out of there, came right home, and locked all of the doors and windows. I haven't been on campus other than for my class since then."

It was evident that Skyler had been traumatized. This guy was a gift served up on a silver platter. Time to get cracking.

"So that's why I always see you around the neighborhood, because you feel safer close to home," Tarantula said softly.

Skyler nodded her head slowly.

"And you keep the doors and windows locked because he knows where you live and you are afraid of what he might do next."

Skyler nodded again. She raised her eyes to meet Tarantula's. There was pure misery there.

"So this jerk is basically messing up your college experience and ruining your life," Tarantula concluded.

"I can't stand it," Skyler whispered in a defeated voice. "I've talked with my parents and my dean, but without any real evidence there's not much they can do. It's his word against mine. They keep telling me to avoid him."

"Well," said Tarantula firmly, leaning back and crossing her arms, "then we'll just have to take matters into our own hands, won't we."

Closer

When she entered her home at 6:00 p.m., Tarantula was feeling quite satisfied with the progress she had made over the course of the day. She almost walked directly into Beelzebub, who was preening in front of the mirror on the wall in the living room.

She took a step backwards and stopped. Not only had he showered and shaved, but he was also wearing a clean and pressed white shirt, dress pants, black leather shoes, and a tailored blue blazer. As she circled behind him, she noted that his hair had been trimmed and carefully combed over the bald spot. She could smell cologne. He was focused on tying a blue silk paisley bow tie while humming to himself.

"What happened to you? Tarantula asked, bewildered.

"Oh, my darling niece, you've returned," he said cheerily, not looking away from his reflection as he dealt with the tricky final loop. "How was your day?"

"My day was great, but apparently not as great as yours. What is going on?"

Beelzebub gave the bow tie one final tug, smoothed his jacket, and turned away from the mirror to face her. He was grinning. Even his teeth looked improved.

"I decided that if I am doomed to remain in this body for the rest of the month, it would be wasteful of me not to make the most of it. The good Mr. Smith was in dire need of a wardrobe update, and I was more than happy to oblige. Fortunately, he has sufficient funds for such extravagances."

"You went out and bought new clothes?"

"Certainly," Beelzebub replied jauntily. "And enjoyed a shave, haircut, manicure, pedicure, and facial as well."

"A facial," she repeated.

"Wait until you see the new automobile that will be delivered here tomorrow. I would have driven it home today, but they did not have the convertible model in the color I desired on the sales lot."

"You didn't."

"Oh, I can assure you I very much did. I think Mr. Smith will enjoy the car enormously when he has his body back. Terribly exciting to drive."

Tarantula paused for a moment and then laughed. "Crazy old Uncle B," she said, shaking her head.

Beelzebub strolled over to the couch and sat. "I have a few moments to spare and would enjoy hearing about your progress with the Temptation Project. As you are undoubtedly aware, today is the end of your first week on The Surface."

Perching on the arm of one of the upholstered chairs, Tarantula eagerly recounted the events of the day, beginning with her meeting with prospect number one on the Earl University campus. She shared the main points of Maria's story with him and then explained her plan of temptation in detail. After listening, Beelzebub was more willing to agree that there was a decent chance Tarantula could deliver this victim to Lucifer within the time allotted.

Then she described her startling street confrontation with Skyler, their talk at her house that afternoon, and her potential vulnerability. Beelzebub was again guarded about the prospect's potential.

"Tarantula," he said in a concerned tone, "although there are many people on this planet who believe changing one's sexual identity is a grave sin, in Hell we are much more open-minded. If this young person were to die, she would not be damned for making the choice to live as a woman."

"I know, I know," Tarantula said irritably. "I believe there is a fragility there that I can capitalize on, but I'm not sure how. You were right last night, I'm finding the implementation of the Temptation Project challenging."

She let out a sigh and rubbed her forehead. "When I oversaw the Adolescent Torture Pit, the souls I interfaced with had already been sentenced to eternal suffering. My job was straightforward; I carried out my duties. But up here on The Surface, well, nothing has been determined yet. The fates of these humans are still unknown, and their choices can lead them in countless directions."

Beelzebub waited as she struggled to put into words why this obvious fact was such a problem for her.

She threw her hands out from her sides and said, "I have chosen these two victims because they are pliable; I am confident I can get them to trust me. That will give me the in I need to tempt them. But now that I have heard their stories, I see that they are complicated individuals."

She stopped, fearful of pushing this line of reasoning further. Lowering her voice, she forced herself to continue. "Forgive me for what I am about to say. As much as I am loath to admit it, I … I see good in them."

She cringed, afraid of how violently he might respond.

Beelzebub was surprised to note that Tarantula was actually quaking in those ridiculous boots she wore. He was once again reminded of how inexperienced she was in matters of The Surface.

"Tarantula," he said mildly, "do not be so hard on yourself. As a tempter on The Surface you must be able to identify both the good and evil in your victims in order to determine which behaviors are best to foster. That is not a weakness. Unless, of course, you encourage the wrong type of behavior."

She looked closely at Beelzebub. Was he hinting that he knew about her secret? This conversation had suddenly veered into dangerous territory.

"You are learning," he continued, "what demons who ply their trade up on The Surface have known since the dawn of man. The world cannot simply be divided into good people and bad people. Within each human being lies a great capacity for both deep kindness and terrible cruelty. It is their possession of free will that grants them the ability and the responsibility to choose which path they will pursue over the course of their lifetimes. Our duty is to ensure that they are frequently and convincingly encouraged to consider evil as an appealing option."

Tarantula rapidly assessed Beelzebub's expression, tone, and choice of words. He seemed to be speaking in general terms, and not specifically about her actions. Relieved, she focused harder on processing the information he was trying to convey.

"So, then, regarding Maria and Skyler," she reasoned slowly, "I must identify both the light and the dark natures within them, and then promote the dark."

"Precisely."

"As always, you have given me a lot to think about. Thank you."

"Of course. And now I must be off."

Tarantula looked at him quizzically. "Where are you going?"

"If you must know, I have a date."

"A date?" she said, stupefied. "I thought you were doing everything in your power to avoid the divorcees and widows."

"I do not believe I mentioned anything about spending this evening with a divorcee or a widow. I have recently discovered some degree of pleasure in the company of our local married women. They make for more interesting prey." Beelzebub's eyes sparkled as he uttered this last sentence.

Tarantula stared at him, her mouth agape.

"You are not the only being in this household who enjoys a stimulating temptation project, you know," Beelzebub said. "I must while away the hours in this ghastly body somehow. And, after all," he added with a smile, "I am only human."

With a nod he walked out of the door.

Over the next two weeks, Tarantula met daily with Maria in the mornings and with Skyler in the afternoons. Typically, they spent the time simply talking. At first, she remained quiet, speaking only to encourage them to vent their insecurities and frustrations. But in time, after getting to know them better and winning their trust, she subtly began to offer observations and opinions that were so skillfully spun that the humans absorbed her perspectives and made them their own.

Regarding Maria, it wasn't difficult to decide which weakness in her character to exploit. For her, body image trumped all things. Becoming and remaining as thin as possible was more valuable to her than her friends, family, education, and health. All she required was regular reassurance from Tarantula that once she had lost enough weight, her life would be perfect. Tarantula knew, as was typical of people with anorexia nervosa, that chances were excellent there would never come a time when Maria was satisfied that she was thin enough.

It had been almost too easy to manipulate Maria so that she religiously avoided any food and drink with significant caloric value. Given Maria's athletic background, Tarantula was also able to encourage her to exercise obsessively. In just two weeks, she was satisfied to observe the dark hollows around Maria's eyes, her jutting cheekbones, and the way her collarbones stuck out from underneath her increasingly baggy clothing.

In addition, with minimal coaching, Maria rapidly became adept at lying to and steering clear of anyone who expressed even the faintest curiosity about her eating or her weight. That was why Tarantula was surprised when a young woman stopped her in the hall outside of Maria's dorm room one day as she was dropping by for a visit.

"Excuse me, are you here to see Maria?" the young woman asked.

"Yes, I'm a friend of hers," Tarantula responded.

This was weird.

"Does she seem okay to you?" the woman asked, her voice filled with concern.

"Yes, why?"

"I'm Tess, her RA. I saw her in the bathroom yesterday and she looked really skinny to me. She doesn't leave her room much, and I never see her in the dining hall. Is she all right?"

Pesky wannabe authority figure. Tarantula was willing to bet this resident advisor cherished opportunities to poke her nose into everyone else's business.

"Well, she did have a touch of stomach flu recently," Tarantula said thoughtfully, pretending to care about this buttinsky's concerns. "She's probably lost some weight due to that. I've been bringing food to her room, so that's why you haven't seen her in the dining hall. She's feeling much better now. Thanks so much for checking, I'll let her know you were concerned."

Tarantula tilted her head to the side and trotted out a small smile. She waited until the RA was down the hall before she knocked on Maria's door. It would be prudent to suggest to Maria that she use the bathroom only when the people on her floor were either out of the dorm or asleep.

At midterm, Maria was not only substantially thinner, but she was also weaker. Tarantula suspected that Maria had begun to skip her classes. She needed to make certain that the professor didn't get concerned and start interfering with Maria's promising progress.

"How's your studying going?" she asked nonchalantly one morning when they were lounging in her room.

"Not so good," Maria admitted. "I feel so tired all the time. Sometimes I can't make myself get out of bed."

"What about your classes?"

Maria groaned and rolled over under her covers. "I told my professor that my grandmother died and that was why I've missed so much class time. I said I was keeping up with the work while I dealt with the loss. He bought it."

Tarantula snickered appreciatively.

Maria turned her head and looked at Tarantula. "Do you think maybe I should take in a few more calories each day? I feel like my thinking isn't very sharp, and my motivation is in the toilet."

Like your food used to be, Tarantula quipped to herself. But she had anticipated that Maria might come up with a suggestion like this eventually. After all, she was wasting away.

"Maria," she crooned, "you've done so well with your eating and exercise. Don't you feel really good about your lower weight?"

"Well, yes, my clothes are totally loose now and I can tell I am smaller, but ...."

"It would be such a shame if you gained back all that fat."

At the word "fat" Maria's gaunt face took on a panicked look.

"I definitely don't want that," she answered anxiously. "But I have a midterm paper to write and it's due by the end of this week. I can't imagine how I'll have the energy to get it done."

"Hmmmm," said Tarantula, making her voice glissade down to sound additionally pensive. "Is there anywhere you could find information that might give you some ideas? Perhaps online?" She innocently gestured to Maria's laptop sitting on her desk.

Maria sat up slowly in her bed and listlessly glanced over at the computer.

"I suppose if I did a few searches that might help me to come up with something to write."

She dragged herself out of bed and sat down in the desk chair. Tarantula skittered behind her and peered over her shoulder at the laptop screen. After Maria typed, "Ideas for a paper about the poetry of T.S. Eliot," numerous links to websites came up. Many of them advertised essays for sale. Tarantula felt a warm glow rise in her chest.

"This has been such a tough summer for you, Maria," she said quietly into her ear. "I am sure that your parents will be so proud of your hard work at Earl University, especially when you show them your terrific grade at the end of summer term. Don't be shy about getting some help from the Internet if you need it."

She patted Maria's shoulder.

"I'm going to give you a little time to get going on that essay. It looks like you've found some useful tools here."

She closed the door quietly behind her as she left.

When Tarantula returned the following morning, she found Maria lying in bed playing a video game on her phone.

"How did the writing go yesterday?" Tarantula asked.

"Oh," said Maria, who was distracted by her next move, "I had a burst of inspiration and wrote the whole paper yesterday afternoon. I already emailed it to my professor."

"Fantastic," Tarantula said, enjoying a rush of satisfaction.

Of course, she couldn't be one hundred percent sure that Maria had purchased an online essay and sent it to her professor, but things were certainly pointing in that direction. Tarantula was feeling especially optimistic about Maria's trajectory. Not only would her submission of a well-written, timely midterm paper reduce the potential for interference from her professor, but it would also make Maria a confirmed thief, liar, and cheater. Why, Lucifer would welcome her with open arms.

Insight

Figuring out how to tempt Skyler was turning out to be impossible. She was a disgustingly kind person. Beelzebub had said that all humans had a dark side, but if Skyler did, she was doing a very good job of keeping it hidden.

Tarantula had already spent over a week trying to crack this nut, and time was running out. There were only two weeks left. Making matters worse, Skyler's mother had begun to nose around in Skyler's affairs, especially as they pertained to Tarantula.

On Friday afternoon, while Tarantula and Skyler were hanging out in Skyler's bedroom, the door suddenly swung open with no warning knock.

"Well, here you two are!" said the woman who burst in. "You must be Tula. Skyler talks about you nonstop. I have been so eager to meet you."

She looked like a smaller, fortyish version of Skyler, complete with the same obnoxious cheeriness. The woman reached out to shake hands, but Tarantula quickly evaded this by leaning back in the now tamed pool float and giving her a wave instead. No touching allowed.

"It's nice to meet you, Mrs. Diggs."

"Mom," Skyler said irritably, embarrassed by this intrusion on her privacy, "what are you doing home so early? I wasn't expecting you for another hour at least."

"Yes, well," her mother said breezily, "since it seems you are spending all of your time with Tula now, and as I was getting the sense that you were never going to introduce her to the family, I thought I'd come home a little earlier today and make us all a nice spaghetti dinner. Tula, I hope you can stay?"

Dinner. Spaghetti. She had read about some of the common foods that humans eat. That was the dish with the wormy noodles covered with what looked like clotted blood.

"Ah, yeah, I'm sorry, Mrs. Diggs, but I can't, my uncle is expecting me home for dinner tonight," she said, aiming for a fine misting of regret.

"I'm sure he can get along without you for one night," the mother replied firmly. "I'd be happy to give him a call if you'd like."

Just what she needed, Mrs. Diggs talking to Beelzebub. He would probably try to seduce her.

"No, that's okay, I'll call him."

"Good. Dinner will be ready in an hour." She thumped down the stairs, making a point of leaving Skyler's bedroom door open.

Up until this moment, Tarantula had assiduously avoided any situation that involved eating in front of humans. That was part of the beauty of working the graveyard shift; it spanned no mealtimes, and she was on her own after Paul went home at 1 a.m. If she ate anything at all tonight, she knew she would have to force it back out later. Thinking about that made her squirm.

But spending time with Skyler's family might give her some insight into a weakness of Skyler's that she could take advantage of. It seemed worth the risk. Maybe she would learn something about that creep at Deadham Community College Skyler had mentioned. So far, she hadn't been able to develop any kind of temptation angle using that story. She went into the bathroom and pretended to call her uncle.

All too soon, Skyler's mother was yoo-hooing up the stairs that it was time to eat. Tarantula followed Skyler into the kitchen. The younger sister was seated at the table, engrossed in her phone. She barely bothered to look up when Skyler introduced her to Tarantula. That was a small thing to be grateful for. Dealing with Skyler's parents would be problematic enough.

"Your father has a business dinner tonight, so it's just us four girls," her mother trilled from over by the stove.

Another break. Tarantula sat down in the empty seat next to Skyler. A round plate with a red tangled mess in the center was placed before her. Her nasal slits contracted as repulsive fumes rose from the steaming heap. For some reason, Skyler's sibling was nudging her arm with a round wooden bowl filled with shreds of green material covered by an oily sheen. Tarantula immediately passed it on to Skyler. How could humans have such problems with obesity? The greasy loaf of sliced bread festering in a basket in the middle of the table required evasive action as well. She pretended to take a sip of her water.

"Well, Tula, tell us all about yourself," Skyler's mother chirped as she jabbed her fork into the mound on her plate and began twisting away.

"My parents died in a car crash and I'm here living with my uncle."

There was a silence around the table. Had she said something wrong? Skyler's sister raised her eyebrows while staring at her plate. Skyler glared at her mother.

"Yes, Skyler shared that with me, I am so sorry for your loss," her mother said uncomfortably, "but tell me, what are your plans?"

"To get my GED."

"Yes, dear, but what are your hopes and dreams?"

How satisfying it would be to explain to this prying human the true intentions she harbored for her precious daughter while throwing the contents of her plate across the table and into her face.

"Mom, stop, leave Tula alone, don't ask her a million questions."

Tarantula shot Skyler a grateful look. "Actually, Mrs. Diggs, I'd love to hear some stories about Skyler. She seems like such a perfect person, there must be some faults you can share with me." She followed this up with a chuckle to make it sound as if she was joking.

Skyler's mother readily launched into story after story about her beloved daughter. Alas, they were singularly about what a kind, smart, and caring person she was. Nothing was mentioned about the problems she was experiencing at Deadham Community College.

Tarantula half-listened as she considered her options regarding how to deal with her food. She could only twirl the wretched noodles around her fork for so long. Changing her grip, she used the side of her fork to hack the pasta into smaller pieces, and then pushed them around on her plate for a while. Where was that stupid dog when you needed him? She contemplated how she might shift some of the debris into her napkin.

"Dear, you haven't eaten a thing."

Tarantula looked up. Skyler's mother was eyeing her.

"I didn't want to say anything before, but I'm actually gluten intolerant."

Sometimes her capacity for brilliance surprised even her.

"Oh, my apologies, I should have asked you," Skyler's mother crooned, but Tarantula was sensing that she wasn't sorry at all. "At least have some salad," she said as she reached over for the wooden bowl and held it out to her.

Mrs. Diggs was clearly watching her now. Tarantula accepted the bowl with a weak smile and put it down next to her plate. She took her time digging through its contents, allowing most of what she scooped up to sift back through the tongs. She was hoping the mother would become engaged in the conversation Skyler and her sister were having, but Mrs. Diggs' eyes remained glued on her every movement. Eventually she selected three pieces of lettuce and set them on the corner of her plate. She balanced one on her fork, placed it in her mouth, and chewed steadily while returning Mrs. Diggs' stare.

She had not learned one useful thing about Skyler for all her suffering. After dinner, she quickly made her excuses and headed for the front door. As she turned to close it behind her, she saw that Skyler's mother had followed to show her out.

"Thank you for your friendship with Skyler," Mrs. Diggs said coldly. "She's one of the most giving, loyal people on this earth. She had been through a lot and I don't want to see her get hurt."

"Yes, ma'am," was all Tarantula could come up with before escaping outside.

Once across the street and safely up in her bathroom, she executed the disgusting task of removing the lettuce she had swallowed. As she watched bits of green swirl in the flush of the toilet, she wondered about Skyler's mother's parting comment. Was it a warning? Was she somehow suspicious? She would have to watch her step around the old hag.

The breakthrough came the next day.

"Why don't you ever eat anything?" Skyler asked as she was fixing a salami and cheese sandwich for herself in her kitchen. "You hardly had anything last night."

Tarantula, distracted by something worrisome Maria had said earlier that day about her resident advisor, answered without thinking. "Because if I eat, I have to throw it up."

"Excuse me?" Skyler said.

Tarantula, shaken from her preoccupation, immediately realized her mistake. She was getting way too comfortable with this human.

"Ah, it's, ah … part of my health problem," she explained awkwardly.

"You know, you haven't told me anything about your life," Skyler whined. "You always make me talk about myself. What health problem?"

"Well," said Tarantula, alert to the ever-present need to be as vague as possible, "I think I may have told you this" (she hadn't) "but I have hypothyroidism. It's pretty bad. It affects my skin, so I have to wear this makeup on my hands and face all the time. I always feel cold, so that's why I wear long sleeves and long pants even though it's summer. And it disturbs my digestion. I have to be so careful about what I eat."

"I am really sorry," said Skyler tenderly. "Is that why, you know, you have to wear a wig?"

Tarantula decided to play the sympathy card. She looked down at the floor and nodded. "I always hope that people won't notice this is a wig," she said, twisting in her chair and feigning self-consciousness. She reached up one hand and fingered a few strands of the dry hair. "I guess it's pretty obvious. It's so embarrassing."

"It isn't obvious at all," Skyler said, anxious to make Tarantula feel better. "I tend be more aware of things like wigs. Why is it embarrassing? Do people make fun of you for it or something?"

Tarantula hadn't given much thought to the opinions of mortals concerning her fake hair. But it was clear that Skyler was hoping that she would say yes, so that they would have the shared experience of enduring peer ridicule. Tarantula nodded slowly, keeping her gaze lowered.

"I'd kill anyone who tried to hurt you," Skyler declared.

And there it was. Mrs. Diggs had said last night at the door that Skyler was one of the most loyal people on earth. Of course. Tarantula remembered from her torturing days that any asset a human had, if used in the extreme, could become a liability.

It didn't take much time for Tarantula to wheedle out of Skyler the name of her tormenter and to find online one Joey Williams who was enrolled in Deadham Community College. It was easy enough to call the Registrar's Office on Monday and convince the student worker who answered the phone to share Joey's course schedule. All she had to say was that she was Joey's friend and was planning a surprise party for his birthday. Because it could only be arranged on a weekday, she wanted to make sure it didn't conflict with any of his immensely important classes.

On Tuesday, she talked Skyler into driving her to Deadham Community College in the afternoon for a tour of the campus. She told her she was thinking about applying there after she got her GED. Skyler was beyond happy to imagine that soon she might have a friend at the school.

While Skyler was showing her around, Tarantula timed her request to see the Mathematics Building to coincide with the end of Joey's calculus class. As they approached the modern concrete structure, students began streaming out through the doors. Tarantula had been concerned about how she was going to identify Joey, but it turned out her worrying was unnecessary. There was only one person in the throng who, upon seeing Skyler, stopped in his tracks and stared at her. He was tall and muscular, with a prominent forehead and small pig-like eyes. Tarantula watched as a nasty grin spread across his face.

"Hey, where've you been, Sweetheart?" he catcalled loudly across the crowd to Skyler while cutting across the people in the walkway.

Tarantula looked up at Skyler, who stood frozen in place. As the young man rapidly drew closer, Tarantula stepped boldly in front of Skyler and yelled, "You must be that creep Joey I've heard so much about."

"Tula, no, don't!" Skyler gasped behind her.

Joey reached Tarantula in three strides, then inched closer, towering over her. A few students stopped walking and lingered, curious to see what was going on. Joey lowered his face to hers. "I see you brought your little dog Toto with you," he sneered.

"Listen, you stupid oaf," Tarantula shouted loudly enough for the onlookers to hear while pointing a finger in his face, "if you ever threaten my friend again, I'll make sure you get locked up in a place where you'll never see your favorite kiddie movie ever again."

There were uncomfortable laughs from the growing crowd.

"And I should be afraid of you, you ugly little alien?" he growled, stepping even closer to her.

Tarantula took advantage of this sudden threatening movement to throw her legs up into the air and land hard on her back. Exclamations of "Oh!" and "Did he hit her?" came from the onlookers. Startled and confused, Joey looked around at the now hostile glances coming from the expanding circle of spectators, then looked back at Tarantula lying on the ground. Saying nothing, he abruptly turned and stalked away. A bystander reached down to Tarantula, offering his hand and asking, "Are you okay?"

Tarantula waved away the extended hand and made a show of moving slowly to her knees, then rising with difficulty to her feet. She thanked the onlooker and limped off. As the mob dispersed, Skyler ran after her.

"Tula, you were so brave!" she exclaimed. "I can't believe you did that for me!"

"This Joey guy is an absolute tyrant," Tarantula responded angrily as she hobbled her way back to the parking lot where they had left the car. "Someone's got to stand up to him. We can't just let him ruin our lives."

That was a good touch. She made a mental note to say "our" and not "your" from now on.

During the drive home, Skyler became increasingly agitated.

"I am so sorry he hurt you," she said over and over while shaking her head and pounding the steering wheel. "This all happened because of me. I hate him. If he ever touches you again …."

Tarantula hid her smile. She knew her wings and tail would be bruised for a few days, but it was worth it.

The Setup

Tarantula used the Deadham Community College incident to steadily intensify Skyler's anger and resentment towards Joey. She deftly wove his name into every conversation they had. By Thursday, Skyler was stomping around her house yelling that Joey Williams could no longer be allowed to interfere with their lives.

It was now the end of Tarantula's third week on The Surface, and precious time was running out. Action was necessary. On Friday afternoon, while they were talking as usual in Skyler's bedroom, she advanced her offensive. She again steered the conversation to their problem with Joey and managed to whip Skyler into a particularly strong frenzy. But instead of allowing her to jabber on about what a horrible person he was, Tarantula upped the ante.

"Enough!" she snapped, as Skyler was throttling one of her stuffed animals.

"Huh?" said Skyler, her hands tight around a pink monkey's throat.

"No more talk," Tarantula hissed. "It's time to do something about it."

Skyler gave Tarantula a puzzled look. "Like what?"

"We confront him and make our demands."

Skyler loosened her grip, smoothed the monkey's fur, and gently placed it back on the shelf.

"And what if he doesn't listen?" she asked quietly.

"Then we give him payback."

Skyler sat down on her unmade bed and began picking nervously at her blanket. "Maybe we should get my parents and my dean involved," she suggested meekly.

Tarantula sighed heavily and folded her arms across her chest. "Look, Skyler, have those people been helpful to you so far?"

"Well, not really," she answered hesitantly, "but probably if I told them about what has been going on lately ...."

"No, do not do that," Tarantula said firmly. "This is something between you, Joey, and me. We must show him we're not afraid of him, that we won't let him intimidate us any longer. If we find we need their help, we can always get them involved."

"Well, okay, if you think that's the right approach," Skyler said, her voice trailing off.

"We are two smart, strong women," Tarantula said, striking her palm with her fist. "We can handle him. I will set up a time for him to meet with us."

"Do you think he'll actually come?"

"I can be very persuasive," Tarantula replied.

Later that evening, using Skyler's username and password, Tarantula was able to access the Deadham Community College Online Student Directory. She looked up Joey's contact information. Before leaving for work she sent him an email:

To Joey Williams,

You are to meet us behind the Observatory on the Deadham Community College campus at 9:00 p.m. next Wednesday night. There we will explain to you why it is in your best interest to never harass us again. If you do not show up, you will face consequences of a most serious nature.

Beware,

Skyler Diggs and Tarantula Smith

P.S. Come alone.

Somewhat dramatic, but it should do the trick. She did not copy Skyler on the email.

Fully expecting the creep to ignore their message, Tarantula immediately kicked off the Hassle Joey Campaign. She peppered his inbox with increasingly threatening emails. She posted nasty stories and embarrassing photoshopped pictures of him on social media websites. On Saturday, she rode the bus to Deadham Community College and stapled mortifying flyers about him all over campus. While there, she gained access to his dorm room by pretending to be his sister and left a dead rat under his pillow.

On Sunday afternoon, there was a message from Joey in her inbox. It read, "Enough. Be there 9. You'll be sorry."

Lightweight, she scoffed to herself. He caved sooner than she had expected. She hadn't even gotten to the skunk yet.

Tarantula was feeling upbeat about the way the Temptation Project was progressing as she walked to work Sunday evening. But while changing out register drawers with Melanie, she couldn't help but notice how coolly the girl was acting towards her. For Hell's sake, by now Melanie should have gotten over the minor difficulties they had experienced during their excursion three nights ago. She could be such a drama queen.

Tarantula had been crossing her fingers that Melanie wouldn't remember the parting comment she had made in the employee bathroom after she had helped Tarantula with her makeup. Unfortunately, this was not the case. Last Tuesday, Melanie ambushed Tarantula while she stood behind the cash register. With Paul watching nearby, she asked Tarantula if she would like to go to the mall with her on Thursday, her day off.

"We can get your ears pierced, you know, like we talked about," Melanie squeaked. "Like, it will be fun!"

As Tarantula looked back and forth between Paul's and Melanie's expectant faces, she felt trapped. She reluctantly agreed to go. In hindsight that was unwise.

At 7:00 on Thursday night, Tarantula met Melanie outside the pharmacy, and they walked across the street to the bus stop by the Earl University campus entrance. During the ride to the mall, Melanie blabbed nonstop about clothes, makeup, hair, and her boyfriend of the week. Tarantula's face ached from the chore of constant smiling.

The noise, lights, foul food odors, and general chaos Tarantula encountered once inside the mall pushed her tolerance for human interaction to the limit. Fortunately, Melanie quickly steered her to a jewelry store on the second level. A yellow and black sign in the window advertised free ear piercing with the purchase of any pair of earrings.

While Melanie dangled gaudy selections at her, Tarantula noticed a pair of silver skull studs hanging on one of the displays. Those would do nicely. She plucked the earrings from the rack and followed Melanie over to a woman who was sitting behind a table in the corner of the shop.

"Where do you want them?" the technician asked while straightening the tools laid out in front of her on a square of green felt. Her hennaed, lank hair hung about her face. As she brushed it out of her eyes, Tarantula glimpsed a barbell jutting through her right eyebrow. More torture devices in the name of fashion, Tarantula mused, thinking of the alligator heels now safely buried in a landfill somewhere.

Melanie piped up, "In her earlobes, please." She looked over at Tarantula and made a tiny jump. "This is so exciting!"

"So exciting," Tarantula echoed, widening her eye slits and sitting down on the stool the woman pointed to.

The technician slid on a pair of thin plastic gloves and tore open a foil packet. The odor of alcohol irritated Tarantula's nasal slits. The woman removed a small white square and reached over to swab Tarantula's right earlobe. As she brushed aside the hair covering the lower portion of Tarantula's ear, Tarantula watched her facial expression shift from bored to curious to repulsed. What an idiot she had been to agree to this mall trip. Hadn't she made a promise to herself never to allow a human to touch her? But before she could reverse her course, the woman grabbed hold of her earlobe, gave its scaly surface a swipe with the cold pledget, and jabbed it with a thick needle.

Nothing happened.

She struck harder a second time, still with no success.

Perplexed, the technician seized a gun-shaped instrument from the felt mat and placed it against the resistant lobe. As Tarantula opened her mouth to object, a loud "snap" rang out and the tool broke into pieces in the woman's hand. Tarantula's earlobe, meanwhile, remained unblemished.

"Oh my gosh, like, did you see that?" Melanie shrieked.

The technician was on her feet now, holding out the shattered instrument and glaring at Tarantula. Customers in the store began edging over to see what had happened. How could she have let things go this far? Of course, nothing man-made would penetrate her scales. She had imprudently drawn attention to herself by participating in this detestable outing. An immediate exit strategy was imperative.

Tarantula jumped up, knocking over her stool, and began shouting at the woman. "My uncle told me never to get my ears pierced in a mall! Your cheap tools are defective! This is an outrage! I am never shopping here again."

Leaving the earrings and a slack-jawed Melanie behind, she stomped out of the store, fled the building, and returned to the bus stop. Melanie caught up with her there but said nothing. When the bus arrived, Melanie boarded, sat in a distant seat, and continued the silent treatment. She hadn't spoken a word to her since.

Tarantula glanced over at Paul, who was avoiding eye contact with her. Melanie must have told him what happened. Well, so what, who cared. Her plans were progressing, and she didn't need their help. As Melanie walked away, Tarantula turned and busied herself with straightening the packs of cigarettes on the shelves next to the counter.

A few minutes later, Mr. Handsome walked through the Employees Only door and approached the register. She was surprised to see him in the store at such a late hour.

"May I have a word with you, Tula?" he asked.

She nervously followed him to his office. Was there a problem? Maybe someone had seen her stealing cigarettes. She always waited until after Paul was done with his shift and she was the only one in the store. She had been careful to swipe a different brand each time, so the missing packs would be less obvious.

"Have a seat," Mr. Handsome said, gesturing to the folding chair.

She sat down and anxiously drummed her fingers on her thighs.

"Tula, you have been working in the store for three weeks now," he began. "As you know, in the beginning I was reluctant to hire you because of your lack of experience and references."

"Mr. Hanson …," she began, but he interrupted her.

"Let me finish. You have turned out to be an exemplary worker. As promised, you are punctual, hard-working, and not a complainer. You have not asked for an advance on your paycheck, which will come at the end of the month."

Tarantula stopped the drumming. This wasn't sounding bad.

"You haven't requested any time off. Which is why I would like to offer you a night off tomorrow evening. My wife is out of town and I don't mind doing an overnight shift this week."

A night off? How delightful. She wouldn't mind a break from the drunken Earl University students who were typically her only customers after midnight.

"Wow, Mr. Hanson, thank you," she gushed, sensing the importance of appearing sufficiently appreciative. "That is so generous of you."

"Keep up the good work," he said.

Around midnight, there was a sound at the store's front door. Someone was having difficulty pulling it open. Paul walked over to investigate. Tarantula heard him say, "Do you need some assistance?"

In staggered Maria, using the wall to steady herself. She was pale and gaunt with dark circles under her eyes. Her clothes hung loosely on her body.

Tarantula was surprised to see her. She had spent some time with her that morning, but Maria so rarely got out of bed these days that Tarantula hadn't realized just how emaciated she had become. Surely the end was near.

"Tula, can I talk with you for a moment?" she asked in a hoarse whisper.

Paul looked back and forth between Tarantula and Maria. When Tarantula glared at him, he turned and walked a short distance down an aisle.

"Tula, I'm so sorry to bother you at work, but I am getting scared. I don't think I can keep doing this," Maria said.

Even her voice was weaker, Tarantula was thrilled to note.

"I'm so tired, I don't have much strength anymore. I think I might have taken things too far this time."

Just go back to your room and die already, Tarantula wanted to say. Instead, she crooned, "Maria, I am so glad you came to see me to talk about this. You look fabulous, by the way. We're going to have to make a trip to the mall to get you some cute new clothes. I bet you're a size 0 by now!"

She looks terrible and you know it, the voice in her head chided.

Tarantula went rigid. It had been weeks since her flaw had plagued her; she had been certain she was effectively containing it. Absolutely no interference would be tolerated. Reaching for a pack of cigarettes and a lighter from the shelf next to her, she slid them into her pocket as she walked around the counter.

"Paul, would you mind covering the register for a sec?" she called sweetly. "I need to talk with my friend."

Paul walked back up the aisle. "Sure," he said, glancing at Maria with concern. "Take your time."

Tarantula linked her arm in Maria's and practically carried her out of the door. Rounding the side of the building, she coaxed her down into a sitting position with her back leaning against the wall for support. Then she dropped down beside her.

"Maria, you have come so far. I am really proud of how strong you have been about making your body so beautiful."

"You don't think I'm too thin?" Maria asked.

"No, you look amazing! You're simply feeling a little weak right now. It will pass."

She smiled at that little joke.

"Let me get you a bottle of water."

"Could I have a bottle of Gatorade or something instead?" Maria pleaded. "I think maybe I need some sugar and electrolytes."

Tarantula considered this possibility. Maria did look pretty bad, and she had to make it back to her dorm room. But she didn't want to risk hydrating her too much.

"Actually, I have just what you need." She pulled the pack of cigarettes and the lighter from her pocket. "Smoking will take the edge off your hunger, give you energy, and let you relax. It's great."

"Smoking? I thought that was bad for you. Do you smoke?"

"Sure, at home all the time," Tarantula said, as she pulled the cellophane top off of the pack, extracted a cigarette, and lit it. She inhaled deeply. "Ahhh," she said.

"Well, if you really think it will help, I guess I could give it a try," sighed Maria. "I feel so awful."

Tarantula lit a second cigarette for her. "I promise this will make you feel better," she said, passing it to Maria.

After some minor coughing, Maria seemed to have the hang of it. It probably wasn't her first time, Tarantula noted. She tipped her head back against the wall and blew a smoke ring. It was a shame Maria was too out of it to notice the delicate white skull and crossbones that wavered briefly in the air. Beelzebub had been an excellent teacher.

When Tarantula returned alone to the store twenty minutes later, Paul stared coldly at her. "I hope your friend is okay," he said.

"Oh, she's fine," Tarantula answered lightly. "Thanks for covering the register."

"Don't forget to pay for the cigarettes and the lighter," he muttered as he walked away.

Foolish Flight

Walking home from work on Monday morning, Tarantula was in her best mood since arriving on The Surface. Everything was going extremely well.

Once again, she reviewed the goals that she had outlined in the basement on the morning of her arrival. Let's see. First, souls for Lucifer. Maria was definitely on her last legs. It wasn't going to be long now before she starved herself to death. As for Skyler, Tarantula was priming her for the Wednesday showdown with Joey by making increasingly violent suggestions about how to handle the confrontation. The Temptation Project was right on schedule.

Her second goal was to carefully maintain her disguise. Although there had been a few close calls, no one had seriously questioned her identity. The humans had totally bought the thyroid story. Her acting had been brilliant.

As for her dark secret, yes, the voice had erupted a few times. But she had effectively quashed it whenever it tried to interfere with her planning. She was handling the situation.

Check, check, and check. At work she was stealing right under Mr. Handsome's nose, yet he thought she was Employee of the Year. The night was hers to enjoy with no tedious customers to bother her.

She had everything under perfect control.

As she arrived at the house, she noted that the silver Mercedes convertible was still gone from the driveway. It seemed like Beelzebub hadn't been around for days. Then again, she hadn't been home much either, what with her daily visits to Maria and Skyler, the mall excursion with Melanie, and the trip to Deadham Community College to provoke Joey. She wondered how the married women in the area were holding up.

Tarantula guessed that Maria would still be asleep after her midnight trek to the pharmacy, so she didn't bother to visit her that morning. She spent a couple of hours with Skyler in the afternoon badmouthing Joey. When she returned home, she wandered around the first floor. The kitchen needed cleaning but that could wait. It was her day off after all. She went upstairs, stretched out on her bed, and reached for her phone to play video games. Hours passed.

Late that night she got up to take a shower. She undressed and shuffled into the bathroom. There she listlessly took out her contact lenses, pulled off the wig, and wriggled out of the body suit. It always felt especially good to release her wings. Stretching them to their full length, she examined each one in the mirror. The bruises from last Tuesday's performance with Joey were completely gone. Her tail seemed to be healed as well. She stepped into the shower and scrubbed her scales. The cascading water was scalding yet unsatisfying.

Leaning against the bathroom sink while fluttering her wings to dry them, she asked herself how she could best make use of this precious night. She felt so blah. What she needed was some exercise. Actually, she realized, reaching up to her left wing and letting the supple membrane slip between her fingers, what she craved more than anything at that moment was to fly.

Returning to her bedroom, she pried apart two slats of the blinds covering one of the windows facing the street and looked up at the dark sky. The conditions were perfect. It was a moonless night. Thick clouds obscured the stars. There was only a slight breeze rustling the leaves in the trees.

And Beelzebub was not around.

She leaned back and let the slats close. She deserved a little fun, didn't she? Hadn't she been cooped up in this horribly uncomfortable costume in this tiny house for long enough? The Temptation Project was coming to fruition and soon she would be returning to Lucifer with three new souls if all went as planned. A flight would clear her mind and sharpen her focus. What harm could a short spin do?

She peered between the slats again. There was a ledge outside of the window. She could climb out, take off from the ledge, do a few circles around the neighborhood, then slip back inside. No one would know.

Tarantula wrapped herself in a towel, then toured both floors of the house to double-check that all the blinds were drawn and lights were off. Then she went back to her bedroom, discarded the towel, and opened the window all the way. The screen was sticky, but she was able to jiggle it up. For good measure, she taped a pencil to the sill to make sure the window didn't jam shut on its own. Placing one leg over the bottom edge of the window and then the other, she ducked under the sash (it was beneficial to be small for a change) and balanced momentarily on the ledge. Bending her knees, she pushed off and launched herself into the sky.

Her wings were out of shape and it took a few awkward seconds to coordinate their flapping. Then she was lifting up, up into the night, feeling the warm July air stream past her face, her body, her wings. Her tail streaked out behind her as she used it to steer herself to a tall pine tree a few houses over.

Resting in the topmost branches, she took a moment to look over the city. Most of the windows were dark. It was so peaceful without the humans crawling around. She took off again and did two wide loop-the-loops and a few spirals. How wonderful it felt to feel her muscles power her higher and higher, and then to relax into smooth descents on air currents. She had missed this terribly.

She spotted the steeple of a church nearby. There was a narrow platform around its base. She headed over and landed gracefully on the wooden planks. Looking up, she could see a cross atop the tall spire.

Don't even think about it. She had to give herself a lot of credit; she had been uncharacteristically well-behaved so far. Here she was, a demon from Hell, and she hadn't performed one prank since she had come to The Surface. Well, she had pierced those condoms, but that was weeks ago. She glanced up at the cross again. It was a church, for Lucifer's sake! It would only take a moment. A piece of old rope lying on the platform caught her eye. Well, that was a sign if ever there was one.

Fifteen minutes later she was climbing back into her house. She removed the pencil, pulled down the screen, and shut the window. The experience had been exhilarating in more ways than one.

A Complication

Almost immediately, Tarantula's phone rang.

"Tula are you okay?" an anxious voice asked.

"Skyler, it's 4:30 in the morning. Why are you calling me?"

"Tula, I think I saw someone climb into one of your upstairs windows. For real. Are you in your bedroom? Do you see anyone there? Are you all right? Should I call the police?"

Devil's damnation, Tarantula hissed under her breath. Skyler was always peeping at her. She shouldn't have exited from a window on the front of the house. How shortsighted of her.

"I'm fine, Skyler," she said in an irritated tone. "You must have seen some shadows on the house. Go back to bed."

"No, Tula, really, I saw this big crawly thing climb over the windowsill and into the house. Maybe there is a burglar inside right now."

"Listen, Skyler, I'm exhausted and want to go back to sleep. All of our windows are closed and locked. There is no one here. You must have seen a cat or a raccoon."

"No, I swear, it was bigger than that!"

"Skyler, go to sleep. Do not call the police. We can talk about this in the morning. I am perfectly safe."

"Okay, Tula, but call me if you need help, I'm right here."

"Thanks, Skyler." She hung up the phone.

Okay, okay, no panicking. She looked around the room. The windows were both closed. She would lock them, and then make sure every other window in the house was shut and locked as well. There was no trace of her flight anywhere. Running over to her bed, she pulled back the covers and flattened the pillow, so it looked slept in. The raccoon story was sounding better by the moment. She'd put her disguise on right away. Things were okay. A quick talk with Skyler was all she needed to convince her that what she saw was a nocturnal animal that probably lived in their chimney.

Tarantula waited until 9:00 a.m. then crossed the street to Skyler's house. As usual, after she knocked, Skyler peered through a crack in the door, opened it wider when she saw who it was, and quickly ushered her inside.

"I am so glad you're okay," she breathed.

"Skyler, I'm fine. I'm pretty sure what you saw was a raccoon."

"No, Tula, take a look at this." She ran into the living room and turned on the television. Tarantula followed her.

"This story has been on all the local news stations," she panted.

Staring out from the television screen was a middle-aged man in a blue suit seated behind a desk. He was earnestly saying something about a UFO sighting.

"A bunch of people in the area reported seeing something big flying around last night," Skyler said over the noise of the television. "Everyone is talking about it."

Tarantula could not believe what she was hearing. It had been a pitch-black night! At 4 a.m.! Why would humans be awake and looking up at the sky at that hour?

"And wait, that's not all. You know the Catholic church down the street? Well, they don't know if this is related, but somehow somebody tied the cross upside down on top of the steeple last night."

Tarantula knew she shouldn't have gone that far, but it seemed like such a good idea at the time.

"That's so bizarre!" she remarked, lifting her eyebrows.

"I know, right? And the scariest part is that they think all this happened between 4:00 and 4:30 a.m., right around the time I saw that thing crawling around your window …."

Tarantula tried to interrupt, interjecting, "That was a rac …," but Skyler insisted on finishing her sentence and said, "… so that's why I had to call the police this morning."

"What?" said Tarantula after a sharp intake of breath.

"There were too many coincidences, I wanted to make sure that you and your uncle were safe."

Trusty old Skyler, always taking care of people. What a mess. But there was no way they were going to be able to pin this on her. Beelzebub would be absolutely furious if he found out. She needed to lie low and let it all blow over.

"The police will be coming to your house today to talk with you, so you might want to stick around. I told them you leave for work around 10:45 in the evening."

"Thanks, Skyler, you're such a considerate friend," she said dully.

The police. They were the last people she wanted any attention from. Great goblins, she just had to make it through this day, then everything would simmer down.

Fortunately, Beelzebub didn't show up at the house that morning. Because it was important to get the situation with the police over with, she waited for their arrival and skipped her usual visit to Maria's dorm room. This was also a strategic maneuver, she reasoned. Maria had been in appalling shape when she showed up at the pharmacy on Sunday night. Tarantula hadn't seen her since, but she predicted she would be even worse now. It wouldn't be smart to be seen around Maria's dorm when they found her dead in bed.

At 1:15 p.m. the doorbell rang. She opened the front door to find two men in police uniforms standing outside. One was tall and thin with a mustache that drooped well past the corners of his mouth. The other was shorter and fatter with a completely bald head.

"Miss Smith?" Fu Manchu asked.

Tarantula nodded.

"We're sorry to bother you, but we received a call about a disturbance at your home last night and we'd like to ask you a few questions. May we come in?"

He flashed his badge while Gandhi fished around in his back pocket, dug out his badge with some difficulty, and showed it to her as well. They told her their names, but she wasn't particularly interested in remembering them.

"Please come in," she said and gestured for them to enter the house. It would be important to cooperate with these morons. She led them to the couch in the living room and offered them a seat, but everyone remained standing.

"Your neighbor tells us she saw a large shape of some sort crawl into a window on the second story of your house last night," Fu Manchu stated.

"Yes, that would be Skyler," Tarantula replied, laughing lightly and slapping her thigh.

Maybe the thigh slap was too much.

"She's very dramatic, you know, always coming up with wild ideas." She rolled her eyes and smiled. "We keep our windows closed and locked. I told her it was most likely a raccoon that has been living in our chimney. I've already called an exterminator."

Fu Manchu did not return her smile. "Yes, ma'am, thank you for that information. Your neighbor says she saw it enter your bedroom window. Were you home last night?"

Serious was probably the better way to play this.

"Yes, officer, I was," she said in a more no-nonsense way.

"Were you up in your bedroom?" he asked.

"Alone?" Gandhi chimed in.

Tarantula gazed steadily at the bald police officer for a moment before answering. "Yes, I was alone in my bed all night. I went to sleep around midnight. Skyler woke me up with her phone call at 4:30 a.m. I told her she probably saw a raccoon and that she should go back to sleep."

"Did you see anything unusual? Notice anything outside of your window or in the sky?" Fu Manchu pressed.

"No, officer, as I said, I had been sleeping."

"Right," the policeman said, removing a pad and pencil from his jacket pocket and jotting down some notes. "May we take a look at your room?"

Tarantula led them upstairs to her bedroom. On the way, the officers craned their necks to see as much of the house as possible.

"Do you live here alone?" Fu Manchu asked.

"No, I live here with my uncle, Bernard Smith."

"Was he in last night as well?"

"No, he wasn't."

Wish he had been, she fumed. Then that troublesome flight would never have taken place.

"Where was he?" grilled Gandhi.

It was an effort for Tarantula to keep her loathing in check.

"Out," she said.

The men looked carefully around her room, paying extra attention to the two windows facing the road. At one point, Gandhi called Fu Manchu over to the window on the left. "There's some kind of print in the dirt on this ledge," he said.

Tarantula stiffened. She looked down at her feet. Stupid, stupid, stupid.

After opening the window and lifting the screen, Fu Manchu leaned out to get a closer look. "Damned if I know what that is," he muttered, pulling his head back inside. "It's pretty small, and there seems to be only one toe print."

They took a final look around and headed back down the stairs.

"Pretty hot in here, isn't it, for y'all to have the windows closed?" Gandhi noted.

"I was about to turn on the air conditioning," Tarantula smoothly responded.

The officers stopped at the front door. "Thank you for your time, Miss Smith, we're sorry to have troubled you," Fu Manchu apologized. "If you have any concerns, please don't hesitate to call us." He handed her a business card.

"Thank you, officers," she said. "I'll be sure to take care of the raccoon situation right away."

They nodded and left.

That had gone tolerably well. Tarantula telephoned Skyler, described the police visit, and declared they had all agreed that what she saw last night was most likely a raccoon. Then she spent the rest of the afternoon trying to take her mind off of irritating newscasts, ugly policemen, nosy neighbors, and absent uncles by practicing smoke rings and playing video games until it was time to leave for work that evening.

The Confrontation

Work on Tuesday night was mercifully uneventful. Tarantula did overhear some talk regarding the UFO reports. Two male Earl University students had been blabbing in an aisle about their theories, ranging from a fraternity prank to an alien spaceship. But by the time they placed their items on the counter they had moved on to discussing plans for a toga party later that week. No one would remember that news story in another day or two.

Walking home early Wednesday morning, she glanced at the house across the street from hers. Skyler was probably in there watching her right now. Hell's bells, what a snoop the girl was.

As she climbed the front steps, she felt a thrill of anticipation about the face-off with Joey that would take place at the Observatory that night. This would be a critical turning point for the Temptation Project. She planned to spend most of her day making sure Skyler's hostility towards him was maximally inflamed.

Tarantula paused on the top step and thought about Maria. There had been no word from her since Sunday night. She took this to be a positive sign. Best to stay away.

At last it was 8:15 p.m. Skyler and Tarantula left for Deadham Community College early so they would have time to scope out the area around the Observatory before Joey arrived at 9:00. Skyler anxiously slid behind the wheel of her car and drove in silence. What a rare treat it was not to be forced to listen to her usual yammering. Tarantula used the time to hammer home the necessity of putting an end to the Joey problem once and for all.

Skyler pulled into the student parking behind the Biology building. The Observatory was a short hike up the hill. They hadn't ventured to this part of campus when Tarantula visited Deadham Community College with Skyler the previous week. Now, walking up the steep dirt road, Tarantula could see that the Observatory truly was on the outskirts of campus. Surrounded by woods on three sides, the solitary gray stone building rose from the trees like a dark fortress. In the twilight she could barely make out its dome. An ancient-appearing glass lamp hung over the entrance, casting a pool of yellow light on the granite steps leading to the front door.

They climbed the stairs, tried the door handle, and found it locked. Peering into first-floor windows, Tarantula could see no lights on or movement inside. They retreated and circled around to the back of the building. A single streetlight dimly illuminated an unpaved parking area. No vehicles were there.

"It's creepy here," whispered Skyler.

Tarantula scoffed and said at a normal volume, "I chose this spot because it looked relatively isolated on the campus map. We don't want anyone distracting or interrupting us, right?"

Or seeing two people die, Tarantula added in her own mind. After all, that was the only way her plan would succeed. In order for her to bring Skyler to Lucifer, two things had to happen tonight. One, Skyler must choose of her own free will to commit an act of pure evil. Something would have to make her so crazed with fury that she would kill Joey Williams. Two, Skyler had to kick the bucket also. Tarantula couldn't very well drag a live human down to Hell, could she? She needed Joey to finish off Skyler. A dance of death between them.

It was a good bet that with Joey's history of knife flashing he would come to tonight's little soiree carrying a weapon. Tarantula had purposefully ramped up her messaging to him during her campus campaign so that it sounded increasingly threatening. That was probably why it took only minor prodding to get him to agree to show up. A guy like that couldn't resist the chance to give someone weaker a good beating. He had been baiting Skyler for years.

"Here, take this." Tarantula slowly slid the sharp carving knife she had taken from her kitchen out from under the sleeve of her leather jacket and handed it to Skyler.

"What?" Skyler said, drawing back. "I … I'm not going to take that. That is not why we're here, Tula. You know I don't believe in violence. I'm just going to talk to Joey."

"Well, that may be your plan, Skyler," retorted Tarantula, "but it's probably not his plan, right? Remember what happened to that kitten you heard about. Think about that night at the party a few weeks ago. Didn't he say you needed something cut off? I don't think he was referring to your hair. You should protect yourself."

She tried again to give the knife to Skyler.

"Tula, I am not touching that thing," Skyler asserted. "Put it away. I can't believe you would even suggest that I hold something like that."

"Okay, Skyler, suit yourself, I'm only trying to give you some insurance," Tarantula said in a tone that clearly indicated she thought Skyler was making a huge mistake.

She slipped the knife back up the sleeve of her jacket. The sound of footsteps crunching on the dirt path leading to the building caused them to turn towards one another.

Skyler took in a deep breath, let it out slowly, and said, "Okay, here goes." She squared her shoulders and called out, "Joey, we're over here."

Rounding the curve of the building, Joey Williams stepped out of the shadows into the dim light of the parking area. No one appeared to be with him.

"Hello, ladies," he sneered as he slowly sauntered towards them, his hands in his jacket pockets.

Even in the low light Tarantula could see his eyes were hard and mocking. He stopped about ten feet away from them.

"Th … thanks a lot for coming, Joey," Skyler stammered. "It was really nice of you."

Tarantula could not believe what she had just heard. Where was the outrage she had spent all day stirring up in Skyler? She turned her head and glowered at her.

"Thanks for coming, Joey," he parroted in a mocking falsetto. "The only reason I am here," he uttered in his regular voice, "is because of the stunts you pulled on campus. You'll pay for the dead rat trick."

Tarantula laughed. "What's the matter, unhappy you didn't get to kill that rat yourself?"

"Wait, wait," said Skyler, holding out her arms with her palms facing forward. "Let's try to …."

Joey cut her off. "Tell your pipsqueak sidekick here she better shut her trap."

"But can't we just …," attempted Skyler again.

Tarantula was quick to interrupt her, and at the same time took three purposeful steps towards Joey. "What we're here to do tonight," she growled at him, "is to shut you down."

Joey moved rapidly towards Tarantula. He stopped in front of her and bent over so that his face hovered above hers. "So, I'm supposed to be afraid of you, some ugly little shrimp who comes up to my kneecaps? What's the matter, too much of a dog to get a date, so you spend your time harassing guys instead? You're pathetic, and so is your wannabe girlfriend here."

He straightened up and glared at Skyler. "You were a sorry excuse for a boy when you were a kid, and now you can't even play at being a girl right. You're just some twisted, disgusting thing in drag. People like you make me sick." He spat a wad of mucus towards Skyler that splatted on the ground.

Tarantula took one step closer to Joey so that they were now two feet apart. He towered above her. In a voice quaking with rage she bellowed, "It's pretty clear there's no talking to someone as ignorant, cruel, and vicious as you are. We're sick of your bullying and we're sick of you. People like you don't deserve to exist."

With that statement, she made a show of brandishing the kitchen knife she had stowed up her sleeve.

"Tula, no!" Skyler shrieked from behind her.

At first Joey seemed taken aback, but he quickly regained his composure. "Put down the toy, little girl," he warned in a low voice, "before you get hurt."

With his eyes fixed on Tarantula's, he slid his right hand out of his jacket pocket and flicked open a switchblade. Light glinted off of the knife's polished surface.

Tarantula hissed, "I'd rather end your life than watch you wreck ours." She made a lunge with her knife at Joey that was intentionally slow and awkward.

With his left hand, Joey easily caught Tarantula's wrist below her hand holding the knife. The extra makeup she had applied there before she left home made her scales especially greasy. In one deft movement she twisted her arm out of his grasp and stepped toward him, closing the gap between them. From Skyler's vantage point behind her, she knew Skyler would not be able to see what happened next.

Tarantula brought her now free arm around in a tight arc and jammed the tip of the knife she was holding into her own chest. It easily pierced her leather jacket and shirt, and sank into the cotton wadding she had packed beneath her body suit that afternoon. Even if the point had reached her scales, nothing man-made would have been sharp enough to do them any damage. The wadding was there to hold the knife in place.

She let out a pained, "Uhhhh," and fell backward so that she landed face up on the ground with the knife sticking out of her torso.

"Tula!" Skyler screamed, running over and throwing herself on her knees beside her.

Joey, standing on the other side of Tarantula, began yelling, "I didn't do anything! I swear, I didn't do anything!"

Tarantula reached up and slowly wrenched the knife from her chest while making choked groaning noises. She let the knife fall from her hand into the dirt at Skyler's knees. Then, rolling her eyes back, she flopped her head to one side and feigned unconsciousness.

Next to her, there was a guttural cry that she barely recognized as Skyler's. "You've killed my best friend," she heard her snarl. She listened as Skyler scrambled to her feet, then cracked open an eye slit to see Skyler leap across her body onto Joey, knocking him to the ground.

She just called you her best friend the voice whispered in Tarantula's head.

No, not now, not now, I'm not listening to you, you don't belong here.

Skyler is risking her life for you, the voice continued. *She would do anything for you. Is this what you really want for her?*

There were sounds of a struggle and cries of pain. Tarantula opened her eye slits wider and saw Skyler and Joey clenched in combat on the ground near her.

You could stop this fight right now.

Tarantula's head felt as if it would explode. Leave me alone, shut up, get out! Can't you see that I am trying to save us from being destroyed by Lucifer? There is no other way!

She craned her neck to better view the grappling pair of humans. Was this what she wanted? Did Skyler deserve to die? It wasn't too late to get up and pull them apart ....

The distant sound of a wailing siren shifted her attention. Someone must have seen or heard them and called the police. She couldn't be found at the scene. With swirling dust as her cover, she got to her feet and ran. She sped around the building, down the hill, and across campus to the bus stop. Luckily for her a bus was pulling up just as she arrived. Brushing the dirt from her clothes, she mounted the steps, paid the fare, and moved to a seat in the back.

As the bus pulled away, she glanced through the window up at the hill where the Observatory stood. That was close; too close. Good thing about that siren.

Culmination

The bus arrived at the Earl University stop at 9:50 p.m. There was plenty of time for Tarantula to get home, change into clean clothes, touch up her makeup, and walk to work. As she passed by Skyler's house, she was warmed by the thought that Skyler would never again be peeping at her through those blinds. What she had pulled off tonight was quite the accomplishment.

But as Tarantula made her way to the pharmacy, her sea of triumph gradually evaporated, and anxiety set up shop in the dry hole left behind. While at home she had scanned the newspaper for news about Maria but found nothing. As she passed dark houses on quiet streets, she tried to dredge up some of her earlier satisfaction by imagining the bloody mess the police were now dealing with behind the Observatory. But Beelzebub had warned her not to count her souls before they were damned.

Speaking of Beelzebub, where in Lucifer's name was he? She hadn't seen him for days. He was supposed to be helping her with the Temptation Project, not chasing after married women. The entire situation was unnerving.

She barely nodded at Melanie as they swapped out their register drawers at 11 p.m. How could she find out what was happening at Deadham Community College and at Earl University? If only Beelzebub were around, he could do some spying for her. She should try to locate him. As Melanie walked away, Tarantula absentmindedly reached up, took a pack of cigarettes from the shelf next to the register, and slid it into her pocket. She could use a smoke to calm her jitters. She would ask Paul in a little while if he would watch the register while she went outside for a quick break.

The Employees Only door abruptly swung open and out walked Mr. Handsome. He was headed directly towards her and looking none too pleased.

"Tula, I must speak with you immediately," he said, his speech clipped. "Please follow me to my office. Paul, would you handle the register?"

Paul instantly appeared from one of the aisles. "Will do, Mr. Hanson." He kept his gaze forward and would not meet her eyes.

She followed Mr. Handsome through the Employees Only door, down the corridor, and into his cramped office. There were two metal folding chairs squeezed in across from Mr. Handsome's desk. In one sat Fu Manchu. Oh, for Hell's sake. Didn't these people ever go home to sleep?

"Hello, Miss Smith," he said. "A pleasure to see you again."

What was this all about? And were there only two policemen in this sad little town? Tarantula nodded in his direction and sat down in the chair next to him.

"Tula, I'll be blunt," Mr. Handsome began, taking the seat behind the desk. "One of the employees came to me on Monday morning and shared a concern that you were stealing from the store."

Paul. She had meant to make a big show in front of him of putting money into her register for the pack of cigarettes and the lighter she had taken when Maria came in on Sunday night. Somehow it had slipped her mind. Annoying tattletale. Melanie was probably behind this as well. She would get them back.

"Oh, I can explain that Mr. Hanson. You see, a friend of mine who was very upset came in …."

He waved away her defense and continued. "Because of this, we mounted a security camera above the register on Monday."

Tarantula's mind raced. She hadn't been in on Monday night. That had been her night off, when she allowed herself that ill-conceived flight around town. Let's see, work on Tuesday had been quiet. Had she helped herself to a pack of cigarettes that night? (She now had a pack-a-day habit, thanks for that, Beelzebub. He neglected to mention how addictive tobacco was.) Blast them all, she did not need this aggravation right now.

Mr. Handsome continued in a stern voice. "I reviewed the video footage and saw that you took a pack of cigarettes at 5:07 a.m. this morning without paying anything into the register. That would be considered stealing from the store. Not to mention that it is also illegal for us to sell tobacco products to anyone under the age of twenty-one. I contacted the police to help me understand what my options were as your employer, and Officer Sanders here was good enough to come over this evening to talk with me. As we were discussing the situation, we both watched you on the video monitor just now put a pack of cigarettes into your pocket without paying. I see no recourse other than to fire you and press charges."

Tarantula was rattled. "Mr. Handsome ... I mean Mr. Hanson, if you'll give me a chance to explain ...."

But no great ideas were coming to her. Think, Tarantula. Then she remembered the strategy that had worked so well for her during her first conversation with Mr. Handsome. She began to exhale loudly while raising her shoulders up and down. Then she added some pitiful sniffing sounds. Dropping her face into her hands she moaned through her fingers, "I'm so sorry, it's been a very hard time for me recently, I ... I ...."

She let out a little sob. What she needed was a moment to gather her wits and come up with a way out of this.

"Is it okay if I use the bathroom?" she whimpered. She lifted her head, pushed her lips down, and raised the middle parts of her eyebrows in an expression that was meant to look tragic. Mr. Handsome glanced over at Fu Manchu who flipped a palm up.

"She can't get far," he said.

Mr. Handsome nodded.

Tarantula stood, pivoted around her chair and skulked out of the door. Couldn't get very far, eh? Really, what was the point of staying? The four weeks Beelzebub had given her to complete the Temptation Project were almost at an end. She had lured Maria and Skyler into circumstances that surely would result in making them the two newest denizens of Hell, with Joey thrown in as a bonus. Once she spoke with Beelzebub, she would know when and how they were leaving The Surface. It must be quite soon. She didn't need this bothersome job anymore, and she certainly didn't feel like coughing up stories for the likes of Mr. Handsome and Fu Manchu. All she had to do was stay out of sight until she found Beelzebub.

She went into the employee bathroom and turned on the faucet over one of the sinks. Then she exited, tiptoed to the back delivery door, quietly unlatched it, and ran.

Across the intersection, through the entrance in the stone wall, and onto the Earl University Campus she sprinted. Then she slowed to a leisurely pace to blend in with the few students who were walking along the paths at that late hour. When she reached the gym she was relieved to find it unlocked. Inside, there was a unisex bathroom immediately to her right. She slipped into the room and bolted the door. This would be a quiet place to think. She doubted anyone in the store had seen in which direction she had headed. Mr. Handsome and Fu Manchu were probably still sitting in his office waiting for her to dry her eyes. Suckers.

Her phone rang. She pulled it out of her pocket. It was Maria calling. What? She was supposed to be dead. Viper's vexations, she swore, as she pushed the button to accept the call.

"Tula?" she heard Maria say faintly.

"Maria!" Tarantula responded in a surprised voice. "How are you? I hadn't heard from you, so I thought that maybe you were, you know, gone."

"Tula, I only have a few moments. I'm not supposed to be talking to you. Is there any way you can come see me right away? I know you're working, but this is an emergency."

Well, at least it was an emergency. There was still hope that she was crumping.

"I'm close to the pharmacy," Maria continued. "I'm in the Earl University Medical Center. It's on the western edge of campus. Tenth floor, room 1019. Please, Tula, it's really important."

Hmmm, the hospital. She doubted Fu Manchu would go looking for her there.

"Sure, Maria," she said in a reassuring voice. "I'll be there in ten minutes. See you soon."

Tarantula looked in the mirror, touched up her wig, and left the safety of the restroom. She peered around the door of the gym and saw no one in the area. Disappearing into the inky night, she rapidly made her way across the campus in the direction of the medical center.

A revolving door herded her into the vast lobby of the hospital. She walked across the open space to the information desk against the far wall. There was a placard on a tripod that posted the hours of visitation. She was nowhere close. A woman with cropped white hair who was wearing an employee badge sat behind the desk. "Visiting hours are over," she announced tartly before Tarantula had even come to a halt in front of her.

Tarantula explained that she was Maria's roommate and that her friend had begged her to bring her phone to the hospital. "I'm premed and was studying so hard for my chemistry test tomorrow that I didn't realize how late it was. Can you please let me deliver it? You know how it is, we college kids can't exist without our phones," she said with a smile. "I'll just drop it off with her nurse, and then I promise, I'll leave right away."

The woman eyed her up and down. "Make it fast," she said.

After Tarantula signed in, the woman pointed her towards the bank of visitor elevators. She hurried over, entered an open car, and punched the button for the tenth floor. The elevator hummed upward and came to a stop. As the doors slid open, she was hit in the face by a wave of hospital stench. The odor, a combination of antiseptic, boiled food, and human funk, made her stagger. Stepping out, she steadied herself by gripping the arm of a wheelchair parked nearby.

She glanced down the grim hallway. In the fluorescent light, the pale tiled walls and the speckled floor took on an eerie yellow-green glow. Although it was quiet, she could hear the undercurrent of humming machines and the occasional murmur of human voices. Signs on the walls directed her to room 1019.

She peeked around the door to see who was in the room. The space was crowded with a bed, a nightstand, an L-shaped table, and a chair. There were two IV poles with plastic bags dangling from them. Tubing from these curled down and into the shrunken figure lying in the bed. Maria.

Tarantula entered the room and gently pulled the door shut. Buried in a mattress piled high with white sheets and blankets and surrounded by railings, Maria appeared even more frail than she had in the pharmacy on Sunday night. A green monitor with luminous lines streaming across its screen beeped rhythmically above the hospital bed. As Tarantula crept closer, Maria turned her head and opened her eyes.

"Tula," she breathed, weakly extending an arm with an IV line sticking out of it, "I'm so glad you're here. We don't have much time."

Tarantula liked the sound of that. She drew nearer to the bed and pulled up the lone chair. "Maria, what are you doing in the hospital?" she asked.

"We have to talk quickly. My parents went down to the vending machines near the cafeteria to get something to eat, but they'll be back soon."

"Your parents? What's going on?"

"Oh, Tula, I am so happy you came," Maria whispered earnestly. "On Tuesday, when you didn't visit me in my dorm room, I started to get really scared."

"I'm sorry about that, an issue came up and I couldn't leave the house."

"I figured something like that must have happened when I didn't hear from you for two days. Last night I tried to get to the bathroom, but I guess I was so weak I collapsed in the hallway. I know you told me not to leave my room when people were around, but I was so thirsty I had to get a drink of water. My RA found me on the floor and called Campus Health Services. The next thing I knew I was in an ambulance that took me here."

Maria's eyes filled with tears.

"I feel terrible about not being there to help you," Tarantula crooned. "We'll get you out of the hospital in no time." She was already thinking of ways to circumvent interference from the doctors and nurses.

"No, Tula, listen to me," Maria begged, nervously glancing at the door. "This was actually a good thing. The university contacted my parents, and they immediately flew to North Carolina. They arrived this morning."

Not a favorable development. Maria tried to touch her sleeve but Tarantula kept just out of reach.

"They have been so supportive of me, Tula. I told them everything: how I starved myself, lied to everyone, cheated on my exam, and stole stuff. They listened and didn't get mad. Then they hugged me and said they hadn't realized how much I was struggling and that they would do everything in their power to help me."

Tears began to roll down Maria's cheeks.

"The doctors and nurses have been so nice too. They told me I had been in danger of dying, and that I was fortunate to have been brought to the hospital in the nick of time."

This was great, just great. All of her hard work down the drain. Tarantula looked up at the IV pole and observed that one of the bags held a white opaque substance. They were probably feeding Maria through her veins already. Devil's damnation! Was this situation even salvageable?

Maria pushed herself up on one elbow and looked earnestly at Tarantula, tears streaming down her face.

"My parents helped me to realize that all I needed to do all along was ask for help. I had forgotten there were so many people on campus and at home who I could have talked to about my problems. I mean, besides you, of course. I feel so much better now that I've been honest about my behavior. I was hating myself. I see now I don't have to live that way. It's a huge relief."

You made her suffer terribly, the voice chided.

Can't you see that I am in danger of losing this victim? Get out of my head.

"But Tula," Maria continued, falling back onto her pillow, "the reason I needed to see you right away is because my parents are angry. I mean super angry. I told them about you, and …."

Tarantula riveted her gaze on Maria's bony face. "What did you say about me?"

"Well, I told them that you were helping me to lose weight by teaching me ways to avoid eating, how to decrease my appetite, and strategies for boosting my workouts. They got all riled up and said you were hurting me, not helping me. Then they called you a dangerous influence. I tried to explain that you are my friend, that you were only doing what I had asked you to do. But they don't see it that way."

Tarantula was now on high alert. This was all she needed right now, a pair of meddlesome parents from Idaho.

"They called Campus Police. They said they were going to find you and press charges."

"What?" hissed Tarantula.

A fine thread of smoke escaped from her left nasal slit. Sweet Lucifer in Hell, not this too. She quickly reached over and grabbed the handle of the pink plastic water pitcher that was sitting on the nightstand by Maria's bed. Thankfully there was a small amount of slushy ice in the bottom. She scooped out a handful and shoved it into her mouth, ignoring the searing chill. Nasty, caustic mush. But as Beelzebub had promised, it immediately doused the flame that had sparked in the back of her throat.

"I know, I know," whined Maria, "I told them they were being ridiculous, but I am sharing this with you so that you are prepared just in case. I think the police are going to want to talk to you. If my parents were aware that I phoned you, that you were in my room, they'd probably call Hospital Security."

This was beyond belief. How did she go from being employee of the month to most wanted person in Deadham in the span of three days?

"You have to get out of here now, Tula. I'll do my best to convince them that I'll fully participate in a recovery program if they leave you alone. But I don't know if they'll listen to me."

You tried to kill her and still she is protecting you.

Tarantula leapt out of the chair. If they found her in Maria's room and called Hospital Security, the brilliant Deadham Police Force of two might connect the dots. Then she would have some real explaining to do. Never mind the loss of Maria's soul, she would still fulfill her quota of two souls for Lucifer. It was time to find Beelzebub and leave The Surface, or at least Deadham. Tonight.

"Thanks for the heads up, Maria," Tarantula said, rushing to the door. As she passed through, she looked back. Out of her mouth slipped, "I'm glad you're getting help."

What the devil was that? She slapped herself in the head as she strode to the elevator.

On the way down, the elevator stopped at the fifth floor. Two men deep in conversation stepped in, turned their backs to her, and continued talking. They were both wearing dark blue hospital scrubs and had stethoscopes hanging around their necks.

"The patient waiting in the ED will be a complicated admission. Sure you're up for it?" the taller one asked.

"Yeah," the other one responded. "I was nervous when I started my internship in June because I heard this year would be hell. But so far, I'm hanging in there."

Tarantula scoffed to herself. Humans didn't have the slightest notion of what Hell had in store for them.

But these two boneheads had given her an idea. On her way in to see Maria, she had seen a sign outside of the hospital indicating that the Emergency Department entrance was located around the corner from the front entrance. The biddy at the front desk had forced her to register as a visitor, and in her hurry she had foolishly written down her real name. It would not be smart to retrace her steps through the lobby; someone from Hospital Security might be sniffing around there right now. She would follow these humans to the Emergency Department and leave via that exit instead.

When the elevator stopped on the ground floor, she trailed after the two men. As they wound their way through corridors, the doctors were too engrossed in their discussion to notice the slight figure shadowing them a few yards behind. At the back entrance to the Emergency Department, the taller man pushed a square silver plate on the wall, and two swinging doors flew outward. In slipped Tarantula after the men as the doors automatically closed.

An open area lay before her that was teeming with humans. She plastered herself against the wall to take a moment to get her bearings. In the center of the room was a circular desk filled with men and women in variously colored scrubs talking rapidly to one another or staring at computers. On the far wall hung a electronic screen where patients' names and room numbers were displayed in white lights. Around the margins of the space were multiple doorways closed off by striped pieces of fabric; she could hear cries and moans issuing from behind the curtains. The sharp odor of disinfectant combined with the metallic tang of blood wafted in the air. In the chaos, she hoped no one would pay attention to a small female inching towards the "Waiting Room This Way" sign that pointed to a hallway. She began to sidle over in that direction.

A familiar voice caused her to freeze. Leaning up against the central station was a man in a police uniform talking with one of the medical personnel. The overhead light reflected off of his bald head. Gandhi. Could she not get a break tonight? She dove behind the curtain of the exam room nearest to her. She couldn't afford to encounter any more policemen.

As she fussed with the curtain to ensure it was completely closed, someone behind her said, "Tula?"

She whirled around. Lying on a hospital gurney was Skyler.

She was alive. Way too alive.

"Skyler!" Tarantula whispered, trying to cover up her shock. "I was hoping I could find you. I came as fast as I could."

"Tula, what happened? I thought you were hurt, I thought you were dead! But you look … fine." Skyler eyed her suspiciously.

"Ah, yeah, well, turned out the knife just made a flesh wound," she answered, probably too casually.

"But you … you ran away," Skyler said, doubt stealing into her voice. "You left me."

"Skyler, listen," Tarantula said, drawing closer to the stretcher. "I was so afraid that Joey was going to hurt you, I ran to get help."

"That's not what the police say. They said you got on a campus bus and were seen in town at the pharmacy."

"That was after I got you some help. I was the one who called the police."

Skyler looked skeptical and was about to say something when Tula quickly diverted the conversation.

"Are you okay? I've been so worried about you."

Skyler studied Tula for a moment. Then she smoothed the sheet lying over her body.

"I'm fine, I only have a few scratches, that's all," she replied coolly.

A few scratches? Tarantula had seen Joey pull out that switchblade and watched the two of them grappling on the ground. It was inconceivable that Skyler had gotten away unharmed.

"How is Joey?" Tarantula asked hopefully.

Couldn't there be at least one soul she could take back to Lucifer and save the Temptation Project from abject failure?

"He'll be all right too. He's in the next room with a broken collar bone."

A broken collarbone? That was it?

"If you're wondering what happened, you know, after you made Joey so agitated that he was impossible to talk with, and then provoked him into a fight, and then got stabbed, and then magically ran away," Skyler said in a sarcastic tone, "I'm happy to fill you in. I was so convinced that he had hurt you that I jumped on him and knocked him to the ground. I gave his wrist a karate chop. That made him drop his switchblade and I kicked it out of his reach. Then I made a second strike to his collarbone and broke it. He gave up fighting after that."

Tarantula was trying to process this information. Skyler had overpowered Joey Williams. Skyler knew karate. Both Skyler and Joey were not dead. Skyler was behaving as if she had lost her trust in her.

"But there is one positive outcome from all of this craziness," Skyler continued. "Before the police arrived, who, by the way, were actually called by a student working in the Biology building, I helped Joey sit up and we were able to talk for a while. He's a really unhappy person. His father is an alcoholic who has beaten him his whole life and who hates queer people. Joey hoped that by bullying me his father might like him more."

A smile grew on Skyler's face as she looked down and began picking at the sheet. "Joey apologized to me for how he's treated me all these years. We're going to meet to talk some more tomorrow at the coffee shop on campus."

The coffee shop. This was all too devastating. No souls at all. Lucifer would be livid.

Skyler raised her chin and narrowed her eyes at Tarantula. "I knew I could get Joey to understand about my transitioning if I had a chance to talk to him. But all you were interested in was violence. I think you actually wanted me to kill him."

It was over. She had failed. The Temptation Project was in ruins. Everything was crashing down around her. She slumped against the wall of the cubicle and looked down at the floor.

There was a long pause.

"I did want you to kill him, Skyler. But once it was all happening, I got scared that you would get hurt."

What on earth? Was that the voice in her mind, or did she actually just say that?

Skyler stared at her and then shook her head and looked up at the ceiling. "That's what's so twisted about all of this," she said quietly. "For a moment there, I thought that was what I wanted too. But while I've been stuck in this exam room, I've had a chance to think. I realized that throughout my life, I'm going to be tempted to react, to do things I know are wrong, because at that very moment the reasons will seem to justify those actions. I have to trust my gut, stick to what I believe in, and let my own values, and no one else's, guide my choices. I could never willingly hurt another human being, that is not who I am."

Tarantula's skull felt like it was jam-packed with superheated lava that was about to blow. She could no longer trust the words that were coming out of her mouth. She didn't know what she thought anymore.

"By the way," Skyler added, "the police are outside. They want to talk to you."

Tarantula snapped to attention as her survival instincts kicked in. The police. She had forgotten about them. As Skyler uttered these words, the curtain to the exam room began sliding over, pushed by a hand connected to an arm in a blue sleeve. Gandhi, still talking over his shoulder to someone at the desk, stepped into the cubicle. As his face swiveled around, his eyes locked on Tarantula's.

"You again," he said.

It was all too much. First the problems with the flight. Then Fu Manchu at the pharmacy. Earl University Campus Police were after her, and now she had to deal with Gandhi. Her three supposed victims were all alive and well and singing Kumbaya. She was hemorrhaging sympathy. She could feel a hot fury building inside of her. Wisps of smoke began leaking out of her nasal slits. If she wasn't careful, she was going to burn the place down. She needed to get out of there and fast, but Gandhi was moving towards her, blocking her exit.

Trapped

There was a sudden blaring from the loudspeakers in the Emergency Department.

"Code Blue, Waiting Area. Code Blue, Waiting Area."

Behind Gandhi, a huge commotion began as medical personnel poured out of exam rooms, grabbed supplies, and began dragging a cart down the hallway leading to the waiting area. As Gandhi turned around to see what was happening, Tarantula saw her opening and made a run for it. She ducked under the curtain, dodged people in scrubs, sprinted through the hallway, pushed past panicking relatives in the waiting room, and burst through the exit door into the evening air. She ran by a row of ambulances, down the driveway, across the main road, and into a residential area. Glancing quickly back over her shoulder, she saw Gandhi standing outside of

213

the Emergency Department entrance with his eyes fixed on her. He appeared to be speaking into a radio.

They would be tracking her soon.

Beelzebub, she must find him. She ran deeper into a neighborhood. Among the streetlights she felt exposed. Where could she hide? She certainly couldn't go looking for Beelzebub at their house. That would be the first place the police would check. The wail of a police siren pierced the quiet. That was quick.

Up ahead was a vacant lot with a few gnarled trees and scattered patches of weeds. She ran into the tallest thicket and crouched down. She had to locate Beelzebub before the police caught up to her. What if they searched using ferocious dogs? How did she land in this ghastly situation? Things had been going so perfectly, and then just like that, everything had slipped through her fingers. The Temptation Project was a fiasco. Drat those adolescent humans and their insufferable free will.

She became so overwrought that a flicker of flame escaped from her mouth and ignited the dry grass at her feet. As she began stomping on the quickly catching fire, an ember shot up and landed in her hair.

Because Beelzebub's assistants had spared no expense in outfitting Tarantula for her journey to The Surface, her wig was made of the finest human hair. In no time at all the ember had sparked a small fire on her head. The acrid smell of burning hair filled her nasal slits.

As luck would have it, July had been an extremely dry month in North Carolina that year. The underbrush readily burst into flame. With fire licking at her legs, Tarantula was horrified to note that the bottoms of her pants had already caught fire. Within seconds, flames were leaping up to her shirt while waves of heat induced globs of makeup to melt off of her face and hands. It would only be a matter of moments before her entire disguise burned away completely.

The humans would capture her. She would be exposed as what she truly was. Lucifer had demanded that this never, ever happen, no matter what.

Tarantula stood up, reached her arms to the sky, and desperately cried, "Beelzebub!"

Now, some people say it was an earthquake that struck at that very moment and caused the fissure in the earth's surface to open. Others argue there must have been a water main break of some sort that caused the ground to cave in. But what Tarantula saw in the midst of the fiery blaze was a thin crack that suddenly zigzagged at her feet and quickly widened into a crevice large enough to accommodate a small demon. Above the crackle of the fire she detected the sound of an insect buzzing insistently in her ear. She threw herself off the edge of the earth and into the cleft.

Lucifer Redux

Tarantula was in free fall through a rent in the earth's crust, somersaulting uncontrollably as she struggled to release her wings and tail from the remaining shreds of burning clothing. Once she was able to peel them off, she expanded her wings, caught an updraft, and slowed her descent. Beneath her she could vaguely make out the glint of a darting insect.

The trip through the earth to the conveyor was more difficult without the luxury of an excavated mine shaft. As a fly, Beelzebub was able to easily travel through the tight crevices and twisting narrow passageways, but Tarantula's progress was much slower as she was frequently forced to land in order to climb over boulders and squeeze through cracks. As she made her way downward, self-recrimination ate away at her. How had all three of her victims escaped? Where had she made her mistakes? Why didn't she anticipate the potential for such disaster? But by far, the most harrowing question was, what was Lucifer going to do with her now?

Exhausted and filled with dread, she finally glimpsed up ahead the outline of the stone platform of the conveyor. The air was hot and close as she touched down. It was pleasing to be warm again, but that was little consolation given what she knew was coming. The fly circling her head alighted on the ground a few feet from her. There was a quick shudder of its tiny frame, and then Beelzebub stood before her in his demon form.

"Well, you certainly did make a mess of things up there," he remarked casually, brushing soot from his arms. "At least you chose a reasonable spot to have your meltdown."

He chuckled at his own joke.

Tarantula looked up at him in shock. He didn't even sound upset.

"H-how did you find me?" she asked, her voice trembling. "I thought I was going to be captured for sure."

Beelzebub sighed. "My main purpose in accompanying you to The Surface was to ensure that your true identity was not discovered by humans. I would never have allowed the police to apprehend you. It was fortunate that you chose to run to a vacant lot directly above one of our vents in your final moments of tribulation."

"But you were gone! I hadn't seen you for days. I didn't know where to find you," Tarantula whimpered.

Beelzebub responded swiftly and firmly. "The Temptation Project was your responsibility, my girl, not mine. I will admit that there were times when I was indisposed while possessing the body of Mr. Smith. But I was fully aware of your progress. I must say, things did fall apart rather abruptly in the end."

He began to stroll towards the conveyer.

"I saw the article in the newspaper on Wednesday about the unidentified flying object spotted over Deadham early Tuesday morning, and had my suspicions," Beelzebub continued. "But when I read the second article about the vandalization of the cross atop the Deadham Catholic Church, it became all too obvious what the mysterious UFO was. How you could choose to perform such a reckless stunt during your short stay on The Surface is inconceivable to me."

"If you had been at home I never would have done it," she whined.

Beelzebub was having none of that. "The decisions were yours to make during this project, Tarantula. My role was to provide support when necessary. You can thank me for orchestrating the Code Blue that allowed you to escape from the Emergency Department."

Tarantula stared up at him in surprise. "You caused that?"

"Of course. It was quite simple. After reading the paper and appreciating that things might be getting out of hand, I decided it was time to abandon the body of Uncle B and take the form of a fly, which I much prefer while performing reconnaissance work. I was able to track you to the Emergency Department, where you appeared to be in somewhat of a tight fix. I flew into the waiting area, identified the oldest mortal there, and entered his nasal cavity. During my brief possession of his body, I stopped his heart from beating."

"But Beelzebub," she gasped, "you taught me that no demon must ever physically interfere with the lifespan of a human."

"Do not fret," he said, reaching the conveyor and pushing the call button. "I restarted his heart and exited his body immediately upon confirming that you had escaped your predicament and were safely outside."

A mischievous smile crept to his lips.

"He did receive an unfortunate series of electric shocks from a defibrillator, courtesy of the capable Emergency Department staff immediately after I took my leave. But he survived."

Tarantula barely heard this last comment. She was processing the realization that Beelzebub had been in the Emergency Department while she was talking with Skyler in the exam room. Had he overheard her confession? Did he know about her flaw? This was disaster upon disaster.

She observed him carefully as he spoke. He was relaxed, joking. He wasn't acting like he was angry or disgusted. In fact, he didn't seem worried at all that the Temptation Project was a complete failure and that they would be returning to Lucifer empty-handed and in disgrace.

"Beelzebub," she couldn't keep herself from asking, "aren't you concerned about what Lucifer is going to say about the Temptation Project? We have no souls to bring to him."

"You have no souls to bring to him, my dear," he murmured. "This was really just a lark for me."

A lark. A bit of light entertainment between inciting worldwide conflict. Wow.

"Well, it may have been a frolic for you," she croaked, "but its nonsuccess could mean the end of my existence."

"That is possible," he said thoughtfully as he stepped into the open conveyor and fitted the silver key into its place high up on the panel.

She followed him inside. For a second time she found herself plummeting through the earth next to him in complete silence.

When the conveyor came to a halt, Tarantula began to shiver violently.

"Can I have some time?" she whispered. "Do I have to face him right away?"

"I am afraid you do," Beelzebub replied.

The only other time Tarantula had been taken to see Lucifer, she had been carried against her will in the huge claws of an unseen messenger. Somehow this visit felt even worse. The conveyor door whooshed open, they exited, and she dragged herself behind Beelzebub along a path of glistening mica.

Soon the familiar rock face loomed in front of them. Apprehension surged through her as she eyed the iron door with its twisting serpents. This was not the triumphant return to the Hall of Lucifer she had envisioned for herself.

The door swung open on silent hinges. There was no pitchfork painfully prodding at her back this time. Beelzebub gracefully stepped across the threshold, spread his wings, lifted from the ground, and swooped down into the dark cavern. Opening her quavering wings, she jerkily rose into the air and followed him towards the glowing circle of flame below.

Up ahead, through the sulfurous smoke, she saw Beelzebub land nimbly on the smooth stone outside of the line of fire guards. She watched as they parted to allow his entry. Tarantula landed in the same spot with a hard thud and somersaulted twice before coming to a stop. Lifting her head, she saw that the opening made for Beelzebub had not closed. Forcing herself up on her hands and knees, she crawled through the gap. Filled with trepidation, she glanced upwards.

Beyond the guards, high on his emerald throne, sat Lucifer in all of his glory. He was even more fearsome than she had remembered. The black talons of his right hand were tapping loudly on the arm of his throne. His eyes were locked on hers.

"Tarantula," his voice rumbled, "such a pleasure to see you again, and in such a short time."

Beelzebub stood over to one side, at ease.

"Your Greatness …," she began but her voice quavered and faded out.

Lucifer leaned forward and glared at her through the hazy air. Then he turned his gaze towards Beelzebub. "What is wrong with her eyes?" he snapped.

Beelzebub sauntered over to where Tarantula was kneeling.

"Stand up," he said quietly.

She slowly got to her feet and looked into his face.

"Take your contact lenses out," he murmured.

She reached up and removed one lens and then the other from her eyes as Beelzebub stepped away.

"Disconcerting," grumbled Lucifer.

There was an uncomfortable silence. Lucifer shifted his position on his throne.

"Tarantula, it is my understanding that you have no souls to present to me today. Is that correct?"

"Yes, Your Divine Evilness," she squeaked, trembling.

"I have also been informed that your identity was alarmingly close to being discovered by humans. Is that true as well?"

"Yes, Sire." She could barely get the words out.

"And your Temptation Project was a total catastrophe?"

At this point she only nodded. She waited for the explosion.

"Hmmmm," he said.

As he turned his elegant head towards Beelzebub, the tips of his curved horns glinted in the firelight.

"Prince of Demons, welcome home. We have missed you."

"Thank you, my lord," Beelzebub said, making a low bow.

"You extracted her in a timely fashion from a situation that could have compromised our world?"

"Yes, my king," Beelzebub acknowledged humbly.

"You must know that I am gravely disappointed in the outcome of this undertaking. Throw her at once into the Abyss."

Although she hadn't allowed herself to hope, Tarantula was shocked by the rapidity of Lucifer's decision. That was it, just incinerate her? No discussion at all? No chance to explain what had happened, how hard she had tried, or what she learned in the process? And Beelzebub receives a hero's welcome even though he only gave her a measly month to do the Temptation Project when she had been promised six? Smoke curled out of her nasal slits. Well, she had nothing more to lose.

As she was about to open her mouth in protest, Beelzebub shot her a warning look while shaking his head almost imperceptibly.

"My lord," he said, stepping forward, "will you allow this faithful servant to speak but a moment regarding the Temptation Project?"

"If you must," Lucifer sighed. He sat back and folded his arms across his chest.

"I would like to acknowledge your brilliance in allowing the Temptation Project to proceed in the first place. It demonstrated to all your open-mindedness and your dazzlingly progressive thinking."

Lucifer sat up straighter on his throne. He loved compliments.

"It is true that the Temptation Project did not fare as we had desired," Beelzebub continued. "I was perhaps mistaken in suggesting that we send a demon who was so grossly inexperienced in matters of The Surface to do your bidding there."

Tarantula cringed. This line of argument was not going to keep her out of the Abyss.

"But what the Temptation Project lacked in productivity it made up for in entertainment value. I am the first to admit that Tarantula's decision to risk a flight on The Surface was a poor one, but I do think her placement of the cross upside down on the spire of that church was an amusing affront to our adversaries."

Beelzebub stepped closer to the dais and leaned in. "Remind me to share the story about the condoms later," he whispered conspiratorially.

As he straightened up and stepped back, he said more loudly, "And we should not forget about the good Bernard Smith. Let us imagine what it must be like for him to return after a month-long absence from his life, only to discover that he had purchased a wardrobe of exceedingly expensive apparel not particularly to his taste, as well as an extravagant sports car."

A smile began to emerge on Lucifer's lips.

"He will be wondering at this moment why the clothing and other possessions of a teenage girl now occupy his guest bedroom."

Lucifer's smile broadened.

"And he will soon learn that most of the married women in the area are absolutely furious with him. He will find their husbands even more prickly to manage."

Lucifer chuckled appreciatively.

"The Temptation Project was not a complete loss. We have identified Joey Williams, who will undoubtedly join us in Hell, if not now, then at some point in the near future. There are more women on The Surface who are now guilty of the sin of adultery. These may not have been the successes we anticipated, but they are definite gains."

Lucifer was clearly enjoying himself now. "And what," he said, "do you propose we do with your inexperienced daredevil demon? Surely her poor performance must be punished in some way."

"Do not destroy her," Beelzebub requested. "Tarantula has creativity, drive, and a deep knowledge of adolescents. She may be of use to you yet. Banish her to the Department of Lava Maintenance instead. That should teach her a lesson."

Lucifer paused to consider Beelzebub's suggestion. Tarantula held her breath.

Shrugging his massive shoulders, he sighed, "It shall be so, Beelzebub. You have given me wise counsel throughout the eons and there is no reason why I should not listen to it today. Now get her out of my sight."

"Thank you, my gracious lord," Beelzebub responded, making another deep bow. He strode over to Tarantula, glanced briefly into her eyes, cupped his hand under her elbow, and drew her up into the air and out of the cavern towards the iron door.

As it swung open and they passed through and landed, Tarantula turned to Beelzebub and said, "You saved me for a second time."

He looked down at her and replied, "Third, if you count the Emergency Room. You were extremely fortunate that we happened to encounter Lucifer in good humor at this moment." He took a few steps forward on the path to the conveyor, stopped, and turned.

"Do not test him again."

The Visitor

Lava maintenance was tedious and arduous work. Tarantula was assigned to a remote lava river that frequently backed up and overflowed its banks. It was her responsibility to ensure that a steady current was maintained. This required the regular removal of potentially obstructing boulders. It was lonely toil that involved no creativity. She longed for her days in Lava Pit 103.

While manipulating a heavy rake to fish out the larger chunks of rock, she had plenty of time to think. Her reflections invariably circled back to the Temptation Project.

At first, she was furious about the way things had turned out. She spent countless hours hurling stones against the sides of her isolated cavern, cursing every human she had interacted with during her time on The

Surface. When she was particularly incensed, her shrieks were so loud that loosened flakes of rock from the cavern's ceiling skittered down the walls. Sometimes she deliberately set the surface of the river on fire with her breath. None of these behaviors provided her any sort of release.

With time, her anger gradually subsided. She began using the endless hours tending the river to think more objectively about what went wrong. She had selected two vulnerable adolescent targets who were lonely and afraid. She succeeded in getting them to trust her. She had systematically isolated them from other avenues of support. Her influence should have led them to death and damnation. How had they escaped?

Skyler and Maria, Maria and Skyler. She couldn't stop thinking about them. She had to admit to herself that these two humans had revealed a shocking capacity for courage in the end. She had made the grave error of underestimating their resilience.

You admire them, the voice echoed in her head.

She glanced anxiously around the cavern to confirm she was absolutely alone. Surely no one could hear what she was thinking, not even Lucifer.

You cared about them. You didn't want them to die.

That is so not true. I did everything in my power to make the Temptation Project a success.

You resisted helping them, yes. But you considered it.

Slamming down her rake, Tarantula paced up and down the rocky bank of the river in agitation. Bloody boogers, was she ever going to be free of this debilitating nuisance in her head? Yes, if she was going to be perfectly honest with herself, there were rare times when she felt a vague attachment to her victims, something probably akin to the ridiculous connections humans made with their worthless pets. But she hadn't given in to these momentary weaknesses; they had not impacted her planning. She had done everything she could to get her victims to die, for Hell's sake. Wasn't that proof enough that she was a loyal servant of Lucifer?

Don't you realize what you want by now?

Tarantula let out a screech so loud that its vibrations caused a mid-sized stalactite to separate from the roof of the cavern and crash to the ground only inches from her. Better if it had smashed her to bits. What in the name of all that was wicked was wrong with her? She threw herself on the ground in despair.

Later, she stood and dusted herself off. She picked up her rake and went back to work. All was not lost. She may not have brought any souls to Lucifer, but no one in Hell knew about her secret. She needed a hiatus, to be completely alone, in order to figure things out. Maybe it was a good thing she had been banished to an obscure hole in Hell.

Time wore on. Although misgivings continued to plague her, they occurred less and less frequently. She no longer heard the voice. Her world consisted only of monotonous raking. She began to accept the harsh reality that she would spend the remainder of her existence in this desolate cavern, alone and forgotten.

So accustomed was she to the isolation of her post that she did not notice the sudden swirl of air, or the sound of beating wings created by the demon who landed softly on the ground behind her.

"Hello," a silky voice said.

Tarantula had been wrestling with an especially stubborn boulder. At the sound, she started so violently that she dropped her rake into the river. It sank into the molten rock. She turned around.

"Oh, I am sorry about that. Do not worry, I will make sure you receive a replacement," the demon purred.

She was statuesque and breathtakingly beautiful. In the dim light, her onyx-colored scales had a subtle sparkle. Tarantula observed that her lavender wings were strapping yet delicate as she gracefully folded them against her shapely shoulders. She was as tall as

Beelzebub, but more lithe. She practically floated over to Tarantula.

Tarantula had not spoken to another being in a long time. No one had come to this spot since she had been exiled. "Hell … hello," she stammered.

"My apologies if I startled you," the demon soothed. "Please allow me to introduce myself. I am Lilith."

Lilith. Tarantula had learned about her at some point in the past. She was pretty sure Lilith was an ancient high demon like Beelzebub. If her memory served her correctly, she was infamous for seducing and bringing to ruin countless eminent humans throughout history.

"Tarantula, I have come here to discuss with you a matter of importance," she continued in her mesmerizing voice.

Tarantula stared in surprise. A high demon wanted to have a conversation with her. Lilith knew her name.

"Dismal surroundings, I must say," Lilith uttered softly as she looked around, then coughed politely into her hand.

Tarantula remained silent, too stunned to speak.

"Yes, well, I would like to talk with you about the Temptation Project."

"The Temptation Project?" Tarantula croaked. She thought she would never hear those words again.

Lilith began drifting to and fro in front of Tarantula, gesturing with her lovely arms as she spoke. "I was present in the Hall of Lucifer when you were brought back from your experience on The Surface. I, for one, thought your idea for the Temptation Project was brilliant and your journey to The Surface quite brave. You were a pioneer."

"A pioneer?" Tarantula repeated.

Her mind was dull. Wake up, pay attention.

"Yes, Tarantula, a pioneer," Lilith murmured. "I was dismayed by the poor reception you received upon your return. You may not have brought souls to Lucifer on that particular occasion, but you paved the way for us to consider how to better entice adolescent souls to Hell. I, for one, am not ready to give up on your project."

Tarantula could not believe what she was hearing.

"Beelzebub is a clever demon," Lilith continued, "but he sometimes does not take things seriously enough. He certainly did not provide you with the guidance you required, and allowed himself foolish distractions while you were handling the most difficult of details." She added in a lower voice, "Maybe he should try possessing a woman's body for a change. He might actually get something done."

Tarantula forced herself to speak. "Well, I could have used more help, and I wasn't given much time …."

"Exactly," Lilith cut her off. "I also believe his choice of venue was inappropriate. Why not choose a place where the teenagers are more amenable to temptation? Say, a reform school or a halfway house for recovering drug addicts?"

This was not something Tarantula had considered. She hadn't thought at all about Beelzebub's decisions regarding the Temptation Project. He did save her three times, though.

"If I were overseeing the Temptation Project, I would play a much stronger role in its planning and execution. I am here to determine if you would consider, in more auspicious circumstances, giving the Temptation Project another try."

Tarantula was flabbergasted. This high demon was offering her another chance to prove her worth. Was it possible that she might escape this prison after all? What about her flaw? Would freedom be worth the risk of exposure? She looked around the empty cavern that was now her home. There was nothing for her here but an eternity of raking.

She was defective, she was sure of that now. But an opportunity like this might never come again.

"I will help," she said.

"Most excellent," the high demon replied. Her face was even more bewitching when she smiled. "I will schedule an audience with Lucifer about this. It may be a bit touchy regarding Beelzebub, but I will handle the politics."

She gazed around at the bleak scenery. "We really must get you out of here. In the meantime, ta-ta for now."

With feline grace, she lifted into the air and was gone.

Dazed, Tarantula plunked down on the hard ground. She thought about the years she had spent working in the Department of Torture. Then she considered her experience with the Temptation Project. Although her time on The Surface was brief, she had learned a great deal about humans. She had also been confronted with tough questions about herself.

She picked up a rock and slung it into the river. Skyler had once said something that had deeply unsettled her. What was it? She thought back to their final conversation in the Emergency Department, just before the brainless bald policeman had burst in. Something about values guiding choices.

Tarantula had told Lilith she would help. But she hadn't said who.

THE END

Acknowledgments

A thousand thanks to my early readers who welcomed the antics of a small bronze demon and offered insights that substantially strengthened this tale: Barrett Rollins, Lorraine Egan, David St. Geme, Sarah St. Geme, Maggie St. Geme, Thomas St. Geme, Joseph St. Geme IV, Anna Wells, Joni Clemons, and Lucy Graves.

To Alan Schwartz, thank you for opening my eyes to the bewilderment, tumult, and marvel that is adolescence.

To William Pritchard, who helped me believe I had opinions worth listening to, my endless appreciation.

I am grateful to the staff of Between the Lines Publishing for making my wish to share *The Temptation Project* in book form a reality.

Finally, thanks to my husband, Barrett Rollins, whose wellspring of love, support, and encouragement leaves me breathless to this day.

L.K. White's career spans attending Amherst College and Harvard Medical School, providing patient care with specialties in internal medicine and adolescent medicine, advising undergraduates at Washington University in St. Louis, Duke University, and Wellesley College, and assisting the Arnold P. Gold Foundation in promoting humanism in medicine. She currently lives in Boston with her husband and their two dogs.